NORA'S NOTION

Kathy,
I hope you
enjoy the book.

[signature]

Other books by Richard Chamberlin

A Collection of Short Stories and Poems

The Cybernetic Possum

Drawings and Writing by

RICHARD CHAMBERLIN

HITCHHIKING FROM VIETNAM: SEEKING THE OX

A memoir by

Richard Chamberlin

NORA'S NOTION

A novel
by

Richard Chamberlin

SPINOZA PUBLISHING

Green Valley, Arizona

Published in the United States of America

By Spinoza Publishing

811 W Circulo Napa

Green Valley, AZ 85614

Cover design and typesetting by Daniel Torres

Cover photo © Adam Stone

www.spnozapublishing.com

ISBN: 978-0-9789093-3-8

Author's note

This is a work of fiction. Names, characters, businesses, places, events, and incidents are either a product of the author's imagination or used in a fictitious manner. Any resemblance or similarity to persons, living or dead, or actual events is purely coincidental.

Acknowledgements

Although I have never met him in person, I would like to thank David Sheppard, author of the book Novelsmithing, for helping me turn my raw ideas into book. His online course helped provide the structure I needed to organize my thoughts into plot points and chapters. I would also like to thank the members of my writing groups, two groups in Madison, Wisconsin, and two in Tucson, Arizona, where I have moved. I also thank Richard Calabro for taking the time to read the entire novel and declaring it was ready to go. This page would not be complete if I didn't thank my wife, Judi Torres, for reading countless drafts over the six years it has taken me to write it. A special thanks go out to my stepson Danny Torres for his awesome cover design. Finally, I want to thank Robin Israel for her great proofreading job and finding all my lost commas.

Table of Contents

1	Love Lost	9
2	The Vision	31
3	Silverman Four	45
4	Fried Plantains	53
5	Piña Colada	58
6	The Man of La Manacha	66
7	18-214	76
8	The Ice Queen	88
9	7&7 and a Pack of Smokes	95
10	Predator	106
11	Ménage à Trois	123
12	Scout Mountain	135
13	The Cruel God	146
14	Lava Hot Springs	156
15	Talking to God in Laundromats	173
16	Pummeled Meat	181
17	Tomorrow Never Comes	193
18	Doubting Thomas	205
19	The Wasteland	224
20	Identify the Emotion	240
21	The Temptation of Joshua	254
22	The Sly One	268

1

Love Lost

ON A COOL OCTOBER MORNING IN 1995, Zack Kincaid eased his Pontiac Starchief onto Madison's Beltline for the last time. He hit the gas pedal and the car shot forward as the eight-cylinder engine roared a final farewell to the city.

In his rush to get on the road, Zack had slopped oil on the engine block. Now the acrid smell of frying lubricant wafted back through the ventilation system. He flipped the driver vents closed just as a Bellamy Brothers tune came on the radio.

Zack stroked his mustache, stretched out his long legs and turned up the volume. "I might as well get used to country music," he sighed then started singing along. "…if I said you were an angel would you treat me like the devil tonight? If I were dying of thirst would your love come quench me…?" He steered to the left of a lumbering semi and tapped the gas pedal. The engine accelerated smoothly. "…if I said you had a beautiful body would you hold it against me?"

He palmed the steering wheel back to the right lane then pushed the cigarette lighter button in and adjusted his sunglasses. When the lighter popped out, he pressed the red hot coil to his cigarette and took a long drag. Tobacco smoke replaced the smell of fried oil.

Zack drove through the brilliant red and yellow fall colors of southwestern Wisconsin toward the land of clear mountain streams and wide open spaces. He had a job waiting for him at a mental hospital in Blackfoot, located about twenty miles north of Pocatello in southeastern Idaho.

The heavily loaded car rode a few inches off the ground. He had picked up the 1968 Starchief Executive at a farm auction—a real find. It had an eight-cylinder, 370 horse-power engine and needed attention, but with a little body work, new tires, and a tune-up it was ready to go.

His cat, Otis, doped with a pet tranquilizer, was sound asleep on top of a pile of bedding. He'd adopted the orange and white tabby from his downstairs neighbor. Otis was the runt of the litter who grew into a fine looking feline. Zack turned around to check on him.

"You're the only friend I have," he said, stroking Otis's belly. They both shared a space in time where the past was dead, the future unborn.

After a couple of hours, Zack pulled into a gas station south of Cedar Rapids. He checked the tire pressure and oil level then grabbed some coffee and a roll. Otis was still sleeping. Zack pulled back onto the road, yawned and patted the dashboard. "So far, so good." Ten minutes later, he hit Interstate 80 and headed west. He drove all day through the cornfields of Iowa and Nebraska and pulled into a rest stop for the night. The next day, as he entered Wyoming, the grasslands began to disappear, replaced by sweet-smelling clumps of sagebrush. He turned off the interstate on the other side of Rock Springs, Wyoming, then exited northwest onto U.S. 30 toward Idaho, somewhere he hoped to turn his life around.

Zack had majored in psychology in college, but had run out of money for graduate school. He worked for a while at a half-way house, then was let go when it lost its funding. He saw an ad in a nursing magazine for a job as a "therapy technician" at the state hospital in Blackfoot, Idaho. He sent in his application and, after a brief phone interview, he was hired.

But before he got to Idaho, Zack wanted to stop and see his old flame, hoping for a little romance on the way. Sonya had just quit her job working with a seismographic crew exploring for oil. She was slim with long red hair and a wicked laugh. Recently, Zack decided that if you could combine Janis Joplin with Bonnie Raitt you'd have had a pretty good likeness of Sonya. He met her in Madison when she was hustling pool for drinks and skating with a local roller rink club under the name of Red Sonja. They became friends and sometimes lovers. Zack admired her grit and loved hearing about her adventures. She had moved out west with another boyfriend several months earlier, but was currently living alone and working part- time as a bartender.

It was sunset when Zack pulled into the small motel outside of Montpelier, Idaho, where Sonya was renting a room. Otis was finally stirring in the back seat.

"OK, buddy," said Zack. Otis stretched and yawned. Zack scratched the cat's ears and clipped a leash to his collar. "We're here." He pushed open the door and stepped outside.

Otis jumped down then sat on the bumpy asphalt and licked his paws.

Zack retrieved a bowl from the car and filled it with water from a plastic jug. The red sunset was fading and the air was cool with a fresh scent of sagebrush. "Here you go." Zack placed the bowl on the ground.

Otis crept forward, sniffed the side of the bowl and began drinking.

Zack turned toward the small motel. The asphalt siding was torn and the overhang was beginning to sag. He noticed the glow of a television coming from behind a set of blinds.

"Now, what was her room number?" Zack scratched his head. He yawned, stretched his arms over his head and popped his shoulder joints. "Five. I think it's five."

He knocked.

"Who's there?" It was Sonya's voice.

"It's Zack."

Sonya opened the door. She was wearing a tight black Jack Daniels tee-shirt with jeans and her red hair was tied back in a ponytail.

"Hey, how the hell are you, Zack!" she said, giving him a big hug.

"I'm fine," Zack said. "You're looking good."

"Well, come on in," she smiled. "How in the hell are you?" she said again, looking him up and down.

Zack removed his hand from her slim waist and peered inside. The room had a double bed and a ratty couch. A hot plate rested on top of a small refrigerator next to a stained porcelain sink.

"Nice little place."

"Oh, Zack, it's just a temporary dive. I've been living here for three weeks. I'm trying to get out of this town. It's a filthy stinkin' hole." Her voice was low and a little raspy.

"What happened to the seismo crew?"

"They laid us off. I'm trying to get some unemployment, but they said I didn't work long enough, so I'm screwed. I was ready to move on anyway… busting my ass all day hauling cables over boulders, setting charges. Shit, there were supposed to be five of us but some days there were only three."

"You were living with a guy, weren't you?" Zack asked. "Living in his van?"

"He was such an asshole. I loaned him a hundred bucks and he never paid me back, turned out to be a fucking coke-head."

"That's too bad." Zack thought, *Here we go again.* "Any place to eat around here?"

Sonya removed the rubber band from her ponytail, and her thick red hair fell forward. She looked good, damn good. "I'm not hungry, but we can walk over to the bar where I work. You can buy me a drink and buy yourself a hamburger."

"Sounds good," Zack said, putting on his cap.

They stepped outside. "Ohhh, look who's here," Sonya said as she reached down to pet Otis. "Hey, Otis, it's nice to see you." She scratched his ears. Otis stood up, stretched and rubbed against Sonya's hand.

"He's just waking up. I couldn't leave him in Madison."

"Oh no…oh no…you couldn't leave him in Madison. I had to leave my cat Midnight there." Her voice cracked and she bit her lip.

Zack looked down at Otis. "I hate to do this, buddy, but I have to put you back into the car." Zack slipped the leash off the bumper. Sonya rubbed Otis's belly one more time before Zack put him into the front seat and locked the door.

They walked a couple blocks to the bar, a small stone structure sandwiched between a hunting store and a laundromat. They sat at the bar and Zack ordered two beers and a hamburger.

Zack lit a cigarette. "You seeing anyone now?"

"Zack, I just want to get the hell out of here," Sonya sighed. She glanced at the barmaid who was smoking a cigarette at the other end of the bar, then pulled her stool closer to Zack. "I went home with this guy I met here. The next day this woman comes to my door and starts asking me questions. She asks if I spent the night with a guy named Jimmy and I said, 'Sure, so what?'" Sonya shot another quick look down the bar. ".. and she says, 'He's my ol' man,' and I say, 'I didn't know that. He didn't say anything to me about you.'" Sonya's voice dropped an octave. "So, she looks in my eyes for a long time and finally says, 'You know, I believe you. I'm glad you didn't try to lie to me.'"

Sonya looked around to make sure no one else was listening. "She's about to leave and then she turns back around and pats her pocket. She reaches in and pulls out the handle of a gun and says, 'If you were lying I would have blown your head off.'" Sonya's eyes grew wide with mock terror and she whispered, "Oh, shit, Zack, I thought I was gonna piss in my pants." She began laughing. "I thought I was gonna...piss...in...my... ...fuckin'... pants." She leaned back and looked around the room in amazement. "Can you believe that? Can you see why I want to get out of this shit hole?"

Zack smiled and shook his head. "Yeah, I don't blame you a bit."

He finished his hamburger and bought Sonya a gin and tonic. She beat him in a couple games of pool then they sat down in a booth where Zack gave her a hug and a kiss.

"Mmmm, that feels good," said Sonya. "You always were a great kisser."

Zack ordered another round of gin and tonics.

She rubbed Zack's thigh. "Why don't you and me head back to the motel," she whispered in his ear. "I have something for John Henry."

"Yeah, and John Henry has something for you too."

They downed their drinks and walked back to the motel, let Otis out of the car, and poured some fresh water in his dish. As Zack leaned against the Starchief, Sonya snuggled up against him and began rubbing his chest.

"I'll bet you haven't had much action in a while," taunted Sonya, kissing his neck.

"I'll bet no one has almost put a gun to my head lately either."

"I'm not going to put a gun to your head tonight, but I just might blow your mind."

Zack grinned, plopped Otis back in the car and followed Sonya inside.

She closed the door and locked the deadbolt.

"I'll be just a minute," said Zack. He used the toilet then checked his wallet. The silver condom packet was still safely tucked inside.

He glanced through the half-opened bathroom doorway and saw Sonya standing next to the bed pulling off her jeans. She had a tattoo on her backside that he hadn't seen before and Zack squinted to make it out. It was a small heart with some writing.

"I'm really happy you stopped by, Zack." She was now completely naked. She sat on the bed and turned on the radio. Willy Nelson was singing "Blue Eyes in the Rain."

"I was getting so lonely. There's nothing but losers up here with more package than product, if you know what I mean." She crawled to the other side of the bed.

"I missed you, too." Zack walked to the bed. He took off his shirt then removed his boots and jeans.

A crack of light from the parking lot showed through a slit in the curtain. Sonya had even put on perfume. Her skin was smooth and warm as Zack gently ran his hand over her body. He brushed her hair back and kissed her neck. She moaned and returned the kiss, then slowly moved her lips down his body until he felt a warm wetness close over him. Zack closed his eyes smiled.

"Hey, how about helping John Henry on with his raincoat," moaned Zack

He handed Sonya the silver packet. She tore it open and put the

Trojan on him. He slipped inside of her.

An hour later, they were both exhausted and they dropped off into a deep sleep.

In the morning Zack awoke before Sonya. He lifted up the sheet and stole a peek at the tattoo located on her rear just below the bikini line. It was just two words—*Love Lost*. He felt a moment of tenderness for Sonya remembering that she'd had a tough life, kicked out of the house by her mother at fifteen when her stepfather began paying a little too much attention to her, then forced to live on the streets. Suddenly, he reconsidered because he remembered that whenever he began feeling something for Sonya, she'd ask him for a favor. Then, when she got it, she was gone. He went into the bathroom and turned on the shower. The pipes rumbled as water sputtered from the showerhead and when he tried to wash with soap, it wouldn't lather up. "Freakin' hard water," he said. He gave up, dried off, then woke Sonya.

"Hey darlin' how you doing," he said, patting her backside.

She rolled over and wiped her eyes. "Jesus, could you hand me a cigarette, Zack?"

"Why don't we get some coffee first? I want to hit the road."

He gave her a quick kiss, but she pulled him closer.

"What's the hurry?"

Zack gave her a longer kiss then threw her a pair of jeans. "Here.

Put these on. I'm starving."

After breakfast, Zack let Otis out of the car to stretch and use the litter. He fed him then, scooped him up and put him back in the car. Otis gave an annoyed meow and retreated to his spot in back. He stretched out on a suitcase and began grooming his paws, occasionally glancing out the rear window as a dog wandered through the parking lot.

Zack gave Sonya a hug then climbed into the car. He adjusted his sunglasses and looked up at her. "I was wondering about that tattoo. I haven't seen it before."

"I'll tell you about it sometime."

"Why not tell me now?" He started up the engine.

"How about finding an apartment in Pocatello when you get there?" said Sonya. "We can share the rent."

"Yeah, sure." She had caught him by surprise. "I'll give you a call after I get settled." He glanced over his shoulder and began backing out.

———————◆———————

Nora Fairchild examined her face with a small mirror at her desk in the counseling department at Idaho State University in Pocatello. She had just applied lipstick but somehow it didn't look right. She liked the color, a burnt red slightly out of the ordinary but still within accepted standards for a professional office setting. She dabbed her lips with a Kleenex. One side looked bigger than the other. She puckered then unpuckered them. *There, that's better. Maybe it was just an optical illusion.* She put the mirror away and turned to the stacks of paper on her desk.

It was Friday afternoon and her boss, Dr. Nederman, had asked her to work overtime to help finalize plans for the upcoming Idaho Psychological Convention.

The phone rang. Nora reached across the papers and picked it up.

"Hello, Dr. Nederman's office," she said, hoping it wasn't another schedule change.

"Hello, darling."

Nora was relieved. "Hello, Mother."

"Are we still on for dinner tonight?"

Nora had forgotten about their plans and hesitated. "I guess so."

"Are you sure?"

"Yes, I'm sure."

"All right darling. I'll pick you up in about an hour."

Nora hung up then looked at her desk, shaking her head.

"Why do I always get myself in situations like this?" She stood up and stretched. *Too bad Mary had taken the week off. We could have worked together, but now everything depends on me.*

Suddenly she began to feel faint. She put her hands on her desk and slowly lowered herself into the chair. Her heart began to pound. Nora took a deep breath, put her head on the desk, slowly exhaled, and began to pray. She pictured Jesus placing his hand on her head. The pounding in her chest gradually subsided and she began to breathe normally. She lifted her head and looked around.

"Thank you, Jesus," she whispered. She kicked off her high heels and pressed her toes into the thick carpet.

Dr. Nederman had given her free rein in designing the office, and she had tried to make it look professional, yet relaxed. She'd selected a modest oak laminate desk for herself and a long, three cushioned couch for guests. Recently, she had replaced a dying geranium with a very realistic-looking plastic one. For the wall, she acquired a large, colorful print of a nineteenth century oil painting. The painting depicted four naked nymphs trying to pull a satyr into a pond. It seemed to her like a natural for the counseling office where rumors about illicit affairs were common.

An hour later, Nora jumped when she heard the door open.

"Oh dear, I didn't mean to scare you." Her mother, Rebecca, walked into the office. She had just been to the beauty salon and her newly curled blonde hair fell just below her shoulders. She put her hands on her hips and looked around. "You poor dear, is everyone else gone?"

"That's right." Nora reached down and began putting on her shoes. "I'll have to stop back after dinner to finish up."

———————◆———————

Late Friday afternoon, Dr. Thomas Nederman walked across the Pocatello airport parking lot, returning from a conference. He scanned the horizon. The sun was setting and he could see the contrails of a jet flying into a red orange sky. The plane was barely visible, but he thought it must have been an F-14 Tomcat operating from the airbase near Mountain Home, Idaho.

As the plane disappeared into the southern sky, Dr. Nederman zipped up his jacket and wished he had become a jet pilot instead of a college professor. Instead of attending boring faculty meetings and spending his weekends grading papers, he could have been doing barrel rolls through banks of clouds or cavorting with the babes who flocked to the nightspots around the base, hoping to go home with a real American hero.

He smiled to himself. It was a nice fantasy but he had carved out a comfortable life in academia. What did he have to complain about? He was the Alfred Adler Professor of the Year. He had penned several books on Adler's therapeutic approach. The most recent one, *You're Not as Bad as You Think*, was received favorably by *The New York Times Book Review*. People aren't inferior, he argued in his text. They merely made errors in logic and perception that led them to that conclusion. The job of the therapist was to challenge those perceptions. Yet, the feeling had been building recently that he had boxed himself in. Maybe his life was too comfortable, too safe. At fifty-two, he felt like he needed a change.

He walked to his red Corvette convertible and climbed in. After putting his briefcase on the seat next to him, he adjusted his rear view mirror and put on his sunglasses. He turned the key and gunned the engine a couple times before pulling out of the parking lot.

Nederman headed down the hill toward Interstate 15 then turned south toward the ranchette ten miles out of town where he and his wife, Ann, lived.

He had bought the 'Vette three years earlier from a student who was leaving for Germany. It handled like a racing car on the mountain roads that surrounded Pocatello. He liked the vibration of the gearshift and the rush of wind in his face.

He gunned the engine on straight-a-ways then downshifted into hairpins, enjoying the shot of adrenaline. He had driven the road at least a thousand times but each time it presented a different challenge. In the winter he would play with the snow and ice, sliding until he began to fishtail then slowing down until he gained traction. Once, on a downhill run, he accidentally drifted into the oncoming lane and had to swerve to avoid colliding with a pick-up truck. Another time he skidded on gravel and narrowly missed a deer. But his quick reflexes had always saved him. He glanced in the mirror and was pleased at the gold reflection of his aviator sunglasses and the way his hair blew wildly in the breeze. He was the master of the road. The vibration of the engine on his body was stimulating and he began to feel aroused, while at the same time feeling like there was a hot rock behind his scrotum.

"Damn prostate," he muttered. He downshifted through another hairpin curve. "Too much coffee, gotta cut back, maybe go to decaf."

He screeched around the last curve, down shifted and coasted onto his dirt driveway. He had thought about having it paved over, but the packed gravel and dry conditions made it unnecessary. He slammed on the brakes and skidded a little before coming to a stop then revved the engine before turning it off.

Ann's car wasn't there. *Too bad*, he thought. *We could have had a quickie.* He remembered once, when they were newlyweds, Ann was sitting on the couch after a shower, wearing only a silk bathrobe and watching the news. He bent down and gave her a kiss. She pulled him toward her and soon they were making love on their shag carpet. Spontaneity was the order of the day back then. Maybe it still was. Just as he walked in the house he heard the crunch of tires on the driveway. *Ann, what luck!* He'd surprise her with a long kiss and it would be like old times. He ran into the bedroom and quickly changed into his robe.

She walked in with her hands full of groceries and called out, "Tom, I could use a little help here." He met her in the kitchen.

"Here, honey, let me help you." She handed him two heavy bags full of frozen vegetables that he put in the freezer along with his diminishing hopes for a hot romp.

"Come on out and help me with the water softener salt," Ann called. "And then you can take your shower."

Dr. Nederman looked down. His passion was gone but the burning in his prostate remained.

———————◆———————

"Hurry up, hurry up," Mindy said to her husband as they drove to the Faith Holiness Church's bible study group. "I don't want to be late for the third time."

"Take it easy, honey. We'll make it." Dave turned right and began a gradual ascent up Third Avenue.

"Can't you go any faster?"

"We'll be there in a minute, honey. Actually I feel a little guilty about coming here." Dave stroked his beard. "If Rebecca is really a prophet, we shouldn't be trying to trick her."

"We're not tricking her. We just want to see for ourselves if she has a special gift."

"But how will we know?"

"We just will, Dave, that's all. We just will. When the Lord speaks through someone, you just get a feeling about it. You'll see. Just let the spirit guide you."

They pulled up to a small, white framed house.

"Here we go, for better or for worse," Dave said.

Rebecca Fairchild greeted them at the door. "Welcome. I'm happy to see you could make it."

"Sorry we're late," Dave said.

"That's all right. We haven't started yet."

They walked into the crowded living room and took seats on the couch next to an older woman with stringy gray hair.

"Hi, Evelyn," said Dave. "How's your husband?"

"Oh, he's so much better," Evelyn smiled. "I think everyone's prayers really helped."

"Praise the Lord!" said Rebecca.

Rebecca glanced at a clock on the mantle over the fireplace, then to a painting of Jesus looking up at a ray of light. She scanned the room, picked up her Bible, and smiled.

"Let us pray." She lowered her head. "Dear Jesus, thank you for this gift of fellowship we are about to receive and thank you for healing our sister Evelyn's husband, Willard, who is battling Satan in the form of cancer. We invite you into our hearts and minds and ask for your divine guidance tonight in understanding the words of the Apostles as inspired by our Father in Heaven. Amen."

Rebecca opened her Bible. "I'd like you to turn to the letter from James 1: 2-4."

She waited, then began to read. "Consider it pure joy, my brothers, whenever you face trials of many kinds, because you know that the testing of your faith develops perseverance."

Rebecca put down her Bible. "Isn't that an odd thing for James to write, that instead of feeling pain at misfortune, we should feel joy?" She looked around the room. She counted eight women plus two couples. When the Bible study had begun, it was mostly elderly who came, squinting at their Bibles and running their fingers along the lines of small print. But, lately, Rebecca was happy to see a few younger people showing up.

"I guess that's pretty hard to do," said a woman with large, round glasses. "We're all sinners and we deserve to suffer."

"But that's the glory of the Lord," said Rebecca. "He doesn't want us to suffer through life. He wants us to feel joy in His presence."

An old man with a cast on his foot raised his hand. "'Scuse me, but if God doesn't want us to feel pain, then why did he let my brother run over my foot. He was backing out of my driveway and backed right over my foot. When I yelled, he stopped and pulled forward then smashed into my garage. Didn't have no insurance either. The doctor gave me some pain pills but they just make me want to sleep all day. What am I supposed to do? I've been praying and praying but I'm still in a heap of pain, still got the smashed garage door, too. What's the Lord gonna do about that?"

Rebecca frowned. "I'm sorry that you are in pain, Charlie, but Jesus never said that bad things won't happen. The church has an emergency fund. I'll pass your name to them. As for your pain, Jesus is there with you. He certainly knows something about pain."

She turned back to the group. "Look at line five. 'God gives generously and graciously to all.' That's what makes our love of God the essential element of our lives. He doesn't withhold His love from those who truly need it. He gives generously."

Charlie began to say something, but his wife gave him a stern look.

Rebecca continued. "Do you think that when the Romans threw the Christians to hungry lions they didn't feel fear? Of course they did, but they knew they were only moments away from entering into everlasting love and life in heaven with God. So when God gives you a challenge, thank Him. If you remain faithful you will become a stronger person."

Dave raised his hand. "Excuse me for interrupting, Rebecca, but I have a question."

"Yes, what is it, Dave?"

"I have heard that you have been given the gift of prophesy, and

I need to know if my brother is going to die. He has taken up with the Devil in the form of alcohol. We have tried everything to get him to stop, but nothing works."

Rebecca smiled as she would with a child. "I don't claim to be a prophet but if your faith is strong and you ask God for help He will provide it."

"But I have to know. Can you see my brother getting better?"

"My dear, we do not always know when God will reveal His plan. All I can say is that I shall pray for your brother and, if we all have enough faith in God's plans for our lives, we will surely reap the rewards."

"Amen," said Evelyn.

A short woman with dark hair and a big belly raised her hand.

Rebecca turned to her. "Yes, Peggy?"

"Yesterday I won a whole case of Coca-Cola at the 7-11 on one of those scratch games, you know, the ones with the clouds and the little airplanes on it? Well I was playin' them for a month and never won until I decided to pray. I don't want to tempt the Lord with silly little things like a lottery, but I'm tired of scratchin' off those little cards and getting' wax in my fingernails all the time and not winning anything so…"

Rebecca's smile faded. She looked at her watch. "Oh dear…thank you Peggy…I completely forgot about the time. Let's all join hands and invite the Holy Spirit into our hearts before we leave."

While driving home Dave turned to Mindy and said, "Well, what do you think?"

"I did get the feeling that there was something special about Rebecca. I could see it in her eyes and hear it in her voice. Didn't you see it, Dave?"

"I don't know. She kinda slipped away when I asked her if she has the gift...claimed to be just a humble servant of the Lord." He stroked his beard. "She's just like the rest of us who..."

"She may not know it," Mindy interrupted, "but I believe she has been touched by the Lord. She is definitely someone to watch."

2

The Vision

NORA'S FATHER, EARL, moved to Pocatello in 1969 after serving in Vietnam. He had come from a large Scotch-Irish family in Kentucky and enlisted in the Army to escape the rural poverty. Earl was awarded a Purple Heart in 1966 for wounds he received when an American artillery shell fell short of its target and killed half his infantry platoon. He called the medal his "purple dog." *Why should I live when better men than I didn't?*

He left the Army in 1967 and returned home. He had planned on getting his old job at the paper mill back, but the plant had gone out of business. His father had died during the war, and his mother sold the house and moved in with her sister. Earl had nowhere to go. It was then that the "shakes" began. He had nightmares about explosions and men dying, and would wake up feeling helpless and alone. He sought help at the nearest VA Hospital but although the doctor gave him tranquilizers, the nightmares continued.

To survive, he joined a gang of bootleggers loading and unloading trucks making deliveries from a still to some of the saloons near town. One rainy night he was riding shotgun on a truck coming down from the hills. As they rounded a curve, the load shifted and the truck tipped over. As it tumbled down the steep embankment, Earl was thrown free. The driver was killed, but Earl escaped with only scratches and a bruise. He limped the rest of the way into town, telling no one of the accident. Memories of his "purple dog" returned and he went on a drinking binge. He woke up wishing he had died.

He swore off whisky, said good-bye to his mother, and began riding the rails. He headed west and ended up in Pocatello where he found a job laying track for the Union Pacific Railroad. The job involved removing and replacing ties, pulling spikes, shoveling rock ballast, loading and unloading equipment. It was hard work but Earl was a big man and it paid a decent wage, just what he needed to turn his life around.

The city of Pocatello was divided by the rail yards of the Union Pacific. The west side of the tracks, which had the most stable soil, had become the downtown. It had the best residences and church-es. The east side of town was the Red Light District with saloons that catered to itinerants of all kinds including railroad workers.

Earl moved into a rooming house east of the tracks. He tried to stay away from the saloons and whorehouses, but with a pocketful of change and an empty heart, the temptation proved too much.

He started drinking again and soon was sneaking nips of whisky during work. One day he was driving spikes when the air hammer slipped and landed on the foot of a co-worker. The man fell to the ground writhing in pain as blood gushed from his shoe. Someone reported that they smelled alcohol on Earl's breath and, after a short hearing, he was fired.

The purple dog was taking bites from his soul. After he was ejected from his rooming house for failure to pay rent, he took to sleeping behind bushes. During the day he hustled up odd jobs to buy booze. As fall approached, he knew he would freeze to death if he continued sleeping outside. Then he heard about a new Salvation Army shelter.

Earl arrived at the small brick building around sunset and waited outside. There were others like him wearing tattered coats and wild beards like pictures he had seen of Russian peasants. At eight o'clock the doors opened and the men filed into a small room with wooden benches. A chipped crucifix hung on the wall behind a wooden lectern.

Earl took his seat with about a dozen other men and waited. The warmth of the wood stove in the corner and the smell of burning hickory reminded him of his childhood in Kentucky, and for a moment his mind drifted back to a time when he was a young boy, the smell of fresh bread as his mother took a loaf out of the oven, his father bouncing him on his knee. What a long way he had fallen

Earl was gripped by a deep sadness, and began to cry silently, wiping the tears away with his sleeve.

A man dressed in a blue uniform with a red collar entered through a side door and walked to the lectern. He was a stout man with gold wire-rimmed glasses and large hands.

"Welcome, my brothers," he said. "I'm Major O'Leary." He slowly turned his head and eyed each man with a stern look then cleared his throat. "If you could, please take off your hats."

An old man with a fuzzy gray beard in the back of the room stood up, pulled off his stocking hat and held it at his side. "When do we eat?"

"Yeah, Father, when do we eat?" said an Indian with long hair and a headband.

"First you get the word, and then you get the bread," said the Major with an Irish accent.

A few more men took their caps off, then others followed.

"Let us bow our heads and pray." He led the men in the Lord's Prayer and then told them that God loved them all in spite of their wretchedness. "Now that you have nourished your soul, it's time to nourish your bodies."

Major O'Leary led the men into the dining room. The unexpected aroma of fresh baked apple pie filled the air. Earl had never smelled anything so delicious in his life. In the middle of the room, white sheets covered tables made from long planks of wood and sawhorses. Along the wall to the right, smiling women in aprons waited behind simple card tables with trays of food. On the opposite side of the room, a pot of porridge simmered on the stove. A young red headed girl with a ladle stood next to it, her eyes darting nervously between the large silver pot and the men.

"Grab a plate and let the ladies serve you," announced Major O'Leary. He smiled at the servers. "If there's anything left, you can have seconds."

Earl straggled into the line and picked up a worn ceramic bowl from the pile. It had a ring stain that reminded him of a chipped bowl his mother used to slop the hogs. As he shuffled forward, he snuck glances at the fresh young faces of the girls serving the food. *I will never be a good enough man to have a wife.* Again, tears formed in his eyes. He blinked them away then looked up and saw an angel staring back at him. He tried to smile back but he had not smiled for so long he felt like his face was frozen.

"Hello," said the angel. "Welcome home."

Earl stared into the most beautiful pair of blue eyes he had ever seen. The young woman wore a pink scarf with blond curls spilling out over the sides.

"This is the home of Jesus and you are welcome. My name is Rebecca Miller."

"Glad to meet you."

Rebecca extended her hand. "And your name?"

"Earl, Earl Fairchild." As he touched her soft hand, Earl felt warmth flowing into his body like rain onto a parched field.

"Would you like some soup?" Rebecca gently withdrew her hand. She dipped the ladle into a cast iron pot.

"Yes ma'am."

She filled Earl's bowl and smiled. "Take some bread and butter, too. The spoons are at the end of the line."

Earl nodded. "Thank you, ma'am."

"Call me Rebecca."

"Thank you, Rebecca," he said. As he suddenly remembered how to smile, the edges of his lips turned upward.

He walked to the end of the line and piled slices of bread and butter on top of his bowl, took a piece of apple pie and let another woman pour him a cup of coffee. He sat down with the others.

"Hello," he heard Rebecca saying to the next man in line. "My name is Rebecca Miller. Welcome home."

Over the next few days Earl couldn't get Rebecca out of his mind. He became a regular at the shelter and stopped drinking. He found a part-time job at a service station and found another rooming house in which to live. Rebecca would stop in for gas from time to time and they became friends.

Rebecca had just finished high school before she met Earl and was working as a nurses' aid at St. Anthony's, the Catholic hospital near the center of town. She had a sunny disposition and a gift for giving comfort and encouragement to the sick. It was her father, a Pentecostal minister, who had encouraged her to volunteer with the Salvation Army.

One day Earl became sick with abdominal pains. He went to the doctor, who discovered a cancerous tumor on his colon. His prognosis wasn't good.

When Rebecca found out, she told her father and they decided to see what they could do to help. They brought Earl into the church and placed him before the altar. Her father asked that the Holy Spirit enter his daughter, so that Earl could be healed. Rebecca placed her hands on Earl's abdomen and began to pray. Suddenly she began to shake and Earl felt a warm rush of energy flow from her fingers into his body. She cried out with joy and asked Jesus to drive out Satan and make Earl well again. A moment later Rebecca collapsed and her father lowered her into a chair. When she recovered, they took Earl home with them. The next day his appetite came back and he began eating.

After a week they went back to the hospital for another x-ray of Earl's abdomen.

The doctor adjusted his glasses, slipped Earl's x-ray into the viewer and flipped on the light.

"This is your large colon a week ago." He pointed to a dark mass. He pulled the x-ray out and replaced it with another one. "Here's what your colon looked like yesterday." He pointed to the screen. The dark mass had shrunk to a small grey blotch. "Darndest thing I ever saw." The doctor took off his glasses and rubbed his eyes. "Every once in a while you'll get a spontaneous remission and I guess that's what happened here. You're a very lucky man, Earl Fairchild."

"Praise the Lord." Rebecca threw her arms around Earl and held him for a long time. Earl began to cry.

"Come back in three months for a check-up," said the doctor.

On Sunday, Rebecca took Earl to church where they thanked the Lord for his mercy. After several months, Earl asked Rebecca to marry him. After checking with her parents, she accepted. Earl seemed like a new person. He smiled more and began saving money for his wedding. When he reapplied for his old job with the Union Pacific, he was rehired.

Rebecca and Earl started a family, bringing Nora and her sister Sara into the world, and developing Rebecca's gifts of the spirit. She learned how to interpret visions, for herself as well as those who came to her for spiritual advice. Earl became a conductor and later an engineer on train runs across the barren desert to Rock Springs, Wyoming. When Nora was five her grandfather died, taken by the Lord because his work on earth was finished, according to her mother. With their minister gone, the small group of Pentecostals moved on to other churches. Earl and Rebecca tried out several churches before settling into the Faith Holiness Church of Pocatello.

After work at Dr.Nederman's office, Nora followed her mother in her own car to the Holiday Inn which was located on a bluff above Pocatello. They selected a table overlooking the broad Portneuf Valley and watched the lights of the city twinkle on at sunset as they ate.

Nora had saved up enough money for a deposit on an apartment and had found one near campus. She knew it wouldn't be easy telling her mother she was moving out, especially after her sister had moved out to get married—but it was time. Besides, Nora knew that her mother would still take her out shopping and if she was late coming home from work, her mother would call and make sure she was all right. On Sundays, Nora, her mother, and her father, Earl, would be going to church together.

"I've found an apartment," Nora said after they had finished eating. "I'd like to move in next week."

"Oh dear, this is so sudden." Rebecca put her hand to her chest. "I knew you were thinking about getting your own place...and that's all right...but, is it in a safe neighborhood?"

Nora rolled her eyes. "Yes mother, it's near campus, right off Benton Street."

Rebecca smiled and sighed. "Well, I guess that's good. Do you need any help moving?"

"Maybe you can help me take some boxes over next week."

"Well, good. I'd love to," said Rebecca. She straightened out the wrinkles in her dress, folded her arms on the table and looked at Nora. "Now that we've taken care of that, I have some wonderful news for you."

"Wonderful news?"

"Yes, I've had a vision."

Ever since Nora's mother was a young girl, she had been able to predict the future with uncanny accuracy. Sometimes visions were contained in vivid dreams, other times she saw apparitions, and every now and then, she claimed that she actually heard the voice of God.

"What kind of a vision?"

"It was a vision of you and Kevin," she said slowly. When Nora didn't reply, she moved forward, looked deep into her eyes and said, "You and Kevin are going to be married."

Nora opened her mouth, but at first nothing came out. "Married? To Kevin Jaworski? Are you sure?" She had never been very attracted to Kevin. They were friends in high school, had gone out to movies a couple times, but that was about it. "Isn't he living in California?" asked Nora.

"I couldn't sleep last night, so I went out on the porch to look at the full moon, said Rebecca, ignoring her daughter's question. "I was thinking about your future when I had the vision. You and Kevin were standing together. You both were dressed in white and he was putting a ring on your finger. Suddenly I felt a...a...." she looked up. "A warm glow came over me and then I heard a voice. It said, 'Trust in the Lord, and His will shall come to pass.'" She closed her eyes and smiled. "I've never been so sure of anything in my life."

"But when are we supposed to be getting married? I thought Kevin had moved? Wasn't he going on a mission for the church or something?"

"All I know is that God has a plan for you and Kevin to be together." Rebecca looked at her watch. "I have to get ready for church now. The choir director wants us to practice a few hymns." She rose from her chair and gave her daughter a hug. "I'll pay for the meal. You just sit here and let things sink in. I'm so happy for you. Have faith. We'll talk more about this later."

Sunday morning, Nora walked beside her father as they slowly climbed the steps of the Church of the Holy Spirit. Though she wore a sleeveless yellow dress and low pumps, Nora felt beads of perspiration forming above her lip. Her father winced with pain as he made his way up the stairs with a stiff left leg. Nora took extra care not to walk ahead of him. Earl had retired from the railroad early, after he injured his knee in a fall.

"Hello, Earl," called a man when they reached the top. Nora looked up and saw Kevin Jaworski coming over to help. She was stunned. Was this the sign that her mother's vision was real?

Her heart quickened as she extended her hand, "Oh hello, Kevin."

Kevin pressed her hand between his and said, "It's so nice to see you again." He turned to her father. "How's the leg this morning, Earl?"

"Could be better," Earl answered, resting on his cane for a moment to adjust his tie.

Nora turned to Kevin and smiled, luxuriating in the tenderness of his touch. She felt a sudden intimacy with Kevin that made her blush. He looked much more mature in his suit and tie than the sweat shirted jock she remembered in high school. Maybe he had changed.

"Well, I see you have all the help you need." Kevin winked at Nora. "Nice seeing both of you again." Kevin turned and walked inside.

Nora watched him disappear into the crowd. How amazing, she

thought, that she would see him now…and what was in that wink?

Nora and her father found some seats near the center aisle. Earl took out his glasses and wiped them off with his handkerchief. Nora, preoccupied with thoughts of her mother's vision, focused her eyes on the large mahogany crucifix that hung above the altar behind the pulpit. As a child she thought that maybe one day the man on the cross would open his eyes and call her name. Sometimes she would find herself staring at the cross then quickly avert her eyes, afraid of what would happen if he actually did. Now, the light glistening off the body of Jesus statue made it seem almost alive.

As the choir began filing in to the right of the lectern, Nora spotted her mother coming in wearing a glorious purple gown. Nora waved. Her mother smiled and waved back. She had never seen her mother looking more radiant. Her blond hair was pinned up in back with curls cascading down the sides to her neck. Her face seemed to glow. Although her mother was beautiful, she had an extra quality Nora longed for. It was the strength of character that showed itself in an even temper and a confidence in everything she did. As a teenager, Nora tried to adopt her mother's persona, but she could never measure up. While her mother was good at conversation, even with strangers, Nora would often choke up or begin to stutter.

In an effort to make herself as beautiful as her mother, Nora began experimenting with cosmetics. She and her girlfriends read fashion magazines and studied the faces of movie stars like Cher and Madonna. They collected free samples of rouge, lipstick and eye shadow at department stores and spent hours experimenting. Nora became expert at applying lipstick, so that it formed a perfect line at the edge of her lips. She tried applying mascara, so that it made her eyelashes appear longer without looking cheap and learned how to apply makeup with a brush, so that it blended naturally with the contours of her face. When she was done her face looked like a work of art, but no matter how hard she tried, she couldn't quite match the beauty and radiance of her mother.

After the service began, Nora looked around the room and saw Kevin sitting with his mother to the left and slightly behind her. His eyes were fixed on the minister. She looked away for a moment then felt her eyes drawn back to Kevin. She hoped that they could at least exchange smiles. *Please God, give me a sign.* But the only sound was the drone of the minister's voice and her father's occasional snoring as he fell asleep against her shoulder.

3

Silverman Four

WHEN ZACK KINCAID LEFT MONTPELIER and drove west to Blackfoot, he scanned the horizon for mountains but found only endless miles of hills covered with dry grey sage brush. They weren't like the mountains he remembered from previous visits out west. Those mountains were like the sirens of Homer that beckoned him closer then played tricks with his mind, hiding behind foothills, playing with shadows and changing character as the sun moved across the sky. Mountains were where the spirits lived and Zack was drawn to their power and majestic ruggedness. He wanted to connect with this power again.

A crimson sun was beginning to set over the desert when he turned onto Interstate 15 near Pocatello, where he located a motel for the night.

Although it was getting dark, Zack checked the map and could see that Pocatello was nestled against the mountains and was located in a valley formed by the Portneuf River. He noticed that the river flowed out of the mountains to the west, into the Snake River, which formed a long crescent through the lower third of the state.

Zack snuck Otis into the motel room, stretched out on the bed, and was about to begin reading a brochure he picked up in the lobby when Otis curled up on his chest.

"Tomorrow I'll find us a place to stay," said Zack, stroking Otis's back. Otis twitched his whiskers, closed his eyes and began purring. Zack held the brochure to the side and began reading.

The Shoshone–Bannock Indian tribe inhabited southeastern Idaho and Northern Utah for hundreds of years before the arrival of white settlement. In 1834, a fur trading post was set up nine miles to the north of the present city. The post, an important stop on the Oregon Trail, became Fort Hall. The Shoshone were led by Chief Pocatello, who staged a series of attacks on Mormon settler incursions into their lands in the 1850's. The US Cavalry waged a campaign against the Shoshone, resulting in their relocation to the Fort Hall Indian Reservation. The city got its start after gold was discovered in Idaho in 1860. On July 3, 1890, Idaho became a state and the city received its charter, named after Chief Pocatello. In 1898, another treaty removed 1/3 of the reservation and in 1902 the land rush began"

Otis yawned and jumped off the bed. He walked to the door and meowed.

"Okay, buddy, just a minute" said Zack. He opened the door carefully, making sure that Otis didn't run out, then retrieved the cat box and a bag of litter from the car. After he poured the litter into the box, Otis jumped in and did his business.

Zack rolled himself a joint and resumed reading the brochure, which quoted a personal account of the events leading up to the gold rush and displayed a black and white photo of a long line of wagons.

"All week, trains have been dropping their passengers in the shade of the red railroad hotel: desert-schooners, each with its wake of white dust, have been plying hitherward. Overnight tents have sprung up along the Portneuf River... Smoke rises from the Pocatello assay office. No one has been allowed within the boundary of the reservation, and yet somehow specimens of ore have detached themselves from the hills and are now being assayed. These Mormons, bearded, hard-handed and shrewd are discussing with surprising familiarity the various lands along March Creek and the forks of the Portneuf."

Zack couldn't keep his eyes open. He put the brochure aside, emptied Otis' litter box into a paper bag then went outside to find a trash can. The night was clear and cool with a full moon and the strong smell of sage in the air. He located a trash receptacle near the office then went back to his room.

The next day, he loaded up the Starchief for the final leg of his trip to State Hospital South in Blackfoot. When he arrived, he read the classifieds and found a furnished apartment on the second floor of an older house near the hospital grounds. He unloaded the Starchief as Otis pranced around his new surroundings meowing and jumping on the furniture.

On Monday, Zack reported to the Administration Building to fill out paperwork and begin his orientation.

State Hospital South was located about twenty-five miles north of Pocatello on the eastern periphery of the small prairie town of Blackfoot. Brown treeless hills stood to the east and the old Blackfoot High School to the north. Newer residential neighborhoods were located to south and west. The hospital grounds were landscaped with spruce trees and consisted of a single rectangle of sidewalks that connected five multi-storied buildings. The units in the buildings had names like New Horizons and Stepping Stones, except for the one where Zack was to work. It was merely called Silverman IV—the fourth floor of a building named after a former doctor.

In the early days of the hospital, recovering patients worked on a farm located on the hospital grounds. The farm was used to supplement meals and helped with the hospital's meager budget. Patients were paid small amounts of money they could use to buy personal items. The fresh air and sunshine, combined with a work ethic, helped speed their recovery. Later, the state required the patients be paid minimum wages; consequently the farm closed. The psychiatric community began to rely more on a new class of psychotropic drugs.

On his first official morning of work, Zack had butterflies in his stomach but he was eager to begin his new life. He rang the buzzer next to a gray steel door on the outside of a drab cement building and waited until a male staff member came to open it. They walked up four flights of stairs and through another locked door marked: DO NOT ENTER. AUTHORIZED PERSONNEL ONLY. Inside the door, a red exclusion zone had been painted on the floor across from a glassed-in office, where the night shift was reporting off. There were several people in the room. Zack found a seat in the corner next to an obese gray haired woman wearing a brightly colored smock.

"Hi," he said. "I'm Zack Kincaid, the new therapy tech."

When she didn't say anything, he said, "It's nice to be here."

"Why?" Her voice was gruff.

Zack turned toward a short woman with black curly hair who was giving the report. She wore fish-net stockings with spiked heels and was leaning on a desk. She picked up a metal patient chart, scanned a page then started reading.

Patient couldn't sleep even though we restricted his caffeine at nine o'clock. He was up times three.

Irene closed the chart. "I think we should increase his dose of Haldol. We caught Frank in the shower at around two, singing and masturbating."

"What did you do about that, Irene?" said the obese woman that Zack had been talking with.

Irene smiled, "I sent Jim in and he told Frank to finish up and get back to bed."

"Good job," said the woman in the smock. Everyone giggled a little.

"Yeah, the second time I went in, he still wasn't done so I turned off the shower and threw him a towel," said Jim, a middle-aged man with a bald head.

"Write him up for inappropriate behavior," said the smock woman.

After the report, Zack learned the obese woman with the smock was Marla Hastings, the head nurse. She had been working on the unit since it opened five years earlier and had seen a lot of therapy techs come and go.

"Welcome to Silverman IV," she said. "Where are you from?"

"Madison… ah, Wisconsin."

"Another Easterner." Marla looked Zack up and down. Zack didn't know what to say. He had never thought of himself as an Easterner, and wondered what that meant to Marla. *What are they going to do? Whip out a six-gun and make me dance?*

"Easterners are supposed to be smarter, or that's what they say," said Marla.

"Well, I… ahhh… don't know about that," said Zack.

"I'll bet you went to college, too."

"I'll have to admit that I graduated with a B.A. in Psych from the University of Wisconsin."

"We won't hold that against you… will we, Irene?" Marla turned to the woman in the fishnet stockings, who was filing her nails.

Irene looked up and gave a quick smile. "Oh, no we'd never hold that against him."

Marla reached over and removed a large black binder from the desk. "Here, this is the policy manual," she said, handing it to Zack. "Get familiar with this. You'll learn a lot more about what goes on around here than in psychology books."

"Thanks." Zack stood up to light a cigarette and grabbed a cup of coffee from the percolator in the corner.

"Oh, I almost forgot." Marla handed Zack two keys. "The silver key is for the bottom door lock, the gold one for the top. Make sure you press the button on the wall before you come in or you'll set off the alarm."

The keys were shiny and new. Zack turned them over in his hand, noting they were slightly larger than most keys. He took out a keychain and snapped them into place.

Suddenly, he felt like the member of a trusted cadre, one that was responsible for the awesome job of protecting society. He also felt a little guilty. Had he sold out? He hoped not, yet he couldn't help enjoying a new sense of power over people's lives. What for the patients was a prison, was for him an easily accessible workplace. At last he had become a member of the establishment. He liked the feeling.

4

Fried Plantains

WHEN KEVIN ENCOUNTERED NORA in church, he had just finished working on a volunteer humanitarian project in South America. It had involved helping indigenous people drill a well in an isolated village in central Ecuador, a project sponsored by his college.

After his last exam, Kevin had taken a plane to Los Angeles then to Quito. From there, he had taken a bone-jarring forty-mile bus ride to the small village nestled in the mountains.

Most of the people there lived in small cement block houses without plumbing or electricity. Kevin's crew would work all morning laying pipe, then go swimming at a waterfall in the heat of the afternoon. Some days he would help patch the roof in the orphanage, prepare food, or just play soccer with the children.

One day, after digging a trench, he was sharing a jug of water with a campesino in the shade of a large oak tree. He glanced toward the bottom of the hill and saw a young woman wearing jeans and hiking boots coming up the path. Kevin wiped his face with his shirt and stood up. She looked different from most of the women in the village. Her hair was short and she was wearing sunglasses.

She smiled and Kevin smiled back.

"Hóla, señorita," he said.

"Please, let's talk in your native tongue," she said, extending her hand. "My name is Maria. I am trying to improve my English."

Kevin took her hand. "I'm Kevin Jaworski from California State University. This is my friend, José. We were just taking a break from work." Her hand was soft and warm. He held it for a little longer than necessary, but she didn't seem to mind.

Maria nodded at Jose and they began conversing in Quechua, the original language of the Incas.

"You speak Quechua?

"I was raised in this area." Maria took off her sunglasses; her eyes were blue-green. "I'm what they call Mestizo. My father is Swedish. He met my mother at the University of Ecuador, where she was a research assistant. I'm a grad student there."

"And what is your major?" asked Kevin.

"I decided to major in mathematics. I know it probably sounds boring but…"

"No, no, no….it sounds fine," said Kevin. "I'm a business major myself and, believe me, I wish I knew more about mathematics, especially stock derivatives."

"Oh, derivatives are nothing," Maria giggled. "When we have more time I'll explain them to you."

They stood there smiling.

Maria looked away, her cheeks flushed. "I'm really here to help you and the other volunteers communicate with the workers."

Kevin scratched his head. "Well, my Quechua is a little rusty. We could probably use the help."

"Good," Maria smiled. "I have to check in with Pastor Perez, and then we will all get together and figure out what is needed."

"That sounds great to me."

They shook hands and Maria went back down the hill. When she reached the car she turned around and waved. Kevin watched as her car disappeared.

"Ella es muy bonita." Jose gave Kevin a playful poke.

"Sí," Kevin smiled. "Let's get back to work."

That evening, after a communal dinner at the church, Kevin and Maria met for a stroll through the town. They talked about their families, business and mathematics, and ways to relieve poverty.

———————◆———————

A week after they met, Kevin and Maria went swimming in a small pond at the base of a waterfall. It was near sunset and the long shadows of the surrounding hills cast their gentle curves over the surrounding jungle.

They climbed down a steep embankment covered with large smooth stones until they reached the water. Kevin jumped in and swam to the middle of the pond.

"Hey, come back," called Maria. She gradually lowered herself into the water and swam out to where he was standing. The falls thundered around them, sending a light mist drifting downstream.

She tried to find some footing and slipped.

Kevin reached out gathering her into his arms.

"I've gotcha." He moved his hands down her back and she put her arms around him.

They played in the water for a while, then swam around the falls. They huddled under a ledge as water crashed down in front of them, then swam back to the other side. They climbed out of the water and scurried up the rocks to the car. Kevin put his towel around her and they hugged. "If you come over to my house, we can cook some dinner," he said. "My hosts are gone for the weekend, but I promise to be a perfect gentleman."

Maria smiled. "I would like that very much."

They drove to Kevin's house, which was in a working class neighborhood on the outskirts of town. Dinner was corn pancakes and fried plantains with melons, and strong coffee sweetened with honey for dessert. At dusk they lay together in a hammock listening to the sounds of birds singing and monkeys screeching.

Over the next few months, Kevin and Maria spent all their free moments together going to local festivals and taking side trips into the countryside. After the well project was finished, Kevin couldn't bear the thought of leaving Maria behind, so he decided to take some business courses the next semester in Quito and meet her family. Kevin flew back to California to arrange for his year of study abroad, then went home for three weeks to visit his family in Pocatello.

5

Piña Colada

KEVIN GRABBED HIS KEYS from the dresser and ran out the door. Mrs. Fairchild had told him that Nora had some school supplies she had collected for the children of Quito. When he called Nora to schedule a pick-up, she invited him for dinner.

Nora looked forward to seeing Kevin. As she finished cleaning her apartment for his visit, she remembered the special feeling she had on the steps of the church when he took her hand in his. It was more than friendship. Or was it? There was nothing wrong with being friends. She imagined giving him a long hug at the end of the night, looking into his eyes and perhaps even pressing her lips to his. Would the magic still be there?

She looked through her closet for something to wear, something to help Kevin remember their last night together. She found a red tank top with black sparkles and a scooped neckline. *Was it a little too revealing?* She removed it from the hanger and held it up to the mirror. *The color looks good—picks up the blush on my cheeks.* She adjusted the straps on her shoulder, dabbed some perfume on her neck and whispered. "Maybe God has a plan for us to be together, after all."

She was taking the chicken out of the oven when the doorbell rang. Startled, she almost dropped the glass dish, but recovered and carefully set it on the stove. She glanced at her watch. It was seven o'clock and Kevin was right on time. She smiled and remembered how punctual he had been when they were dating in high school.

She took off her oven mitt and opened the door.

"I hope I'm not too early," Kevin said.

"It's nice to see you." She stepped forward and hugged him, noticing the pleasant scent of his aftershave.

"It's nice to see you too." Kevin glanced down at the tops of her breasts, then looked away. "Thanks a lot for the school supplies."

"I'm just glad I can help." Nora pointed to two boxes stacked in the living room.

"Let me get them loaded before I forget and I'll be right back up."

"That's fine. Dinner is almost ready."

When Kevin returned, he asked if he could help.

Nora went to the cupboard and took out some plates. "Here, you can set the table and I'll get the chicken ready."

Dinner conversation revolved around Kevin's summer project and his plans to study abroad. After dinner, they sat on the couch and looked at Nora's high school yearbook.

Kevin held the book and Nora scooted closer to him.

"Look here." She pointed to Kevin in his football uniform and rubbed her bare arm against his. "You were such a handsome quarterback. I'll bet you had your pick of girlfriends."

"No, not really."

"You could have fooled me." Nora leaned forward to look at Kevin directly. "What about that little blond cheerleader, Suzie? What was her last name? You two were pretty tight for a while." She poked him playfully.

Kevin grimaced. "Yeah, Susie Culver dumped me at the end of the football season. I was talking about going to seminary back then and I guess she decided she didn't want to become a preacher's wife."

"I'm sorry. I didn't mean to make you feel bad."

"Oh no, I'm okay with that now. I decided to major in business, but I'm still interested in working with the church. That's why I went to Ecuador. I guess that just turns some people off."

They exchanged smiles.

Nora kissed him on the cheek.

"I want you to know that I admire a man who acts from his heart," she whispered.

Kevin blushed. "I always liked you, Nora. I liked you a lot. It just seemed you were always inaccessible."

"I'm not inaccessible now." Nora moved her hand over Kevin's shoulders feeling the curve of his muscles. She felt her nipples get hard and her heart began to pound.

Kevin leaned forward, lowered his head and smiled. "I've really enjoyed seeing you again but I have to leave pretty soon—big day tomorrow."

"Of course you do," said Nora, rubbing Kevin's neck. "I wish we had more time together, too." She moved her hand lower and gently traced circles on his back with her fingernails.

"That feels great," Kevin said.

Nora slipped her hand under his shirt.

Kevin pulled away. "I should probably get going."

Nora removed her hand. *Oh no*, she thought, *I've gone too far.*

"Are you sure? I could fix us a drink."

The phone next to the couch rang but Nora ignored it. "How about a margarita? They must make margaritas in Ecuador."

Kevin looked at the phone. "Aren't you going to answer it?"

Nora picked up the receiver. "I can't talk now, Mother. Yes, Kevin is here. Yes, I'll call you back later. Goodbye."

Kevin had gotten up and was headed to the door.

Nora followed him and he stopped to give her a hug. "It was great seeing you again."

"Maybe we can catch a movie before you leave."

"Sounds great, I'll give you a call."

Nora watched Kevin's car drive away until his red tail lights disappeared into the night. She went back inside. Her body felt empty as she picked up the telephone then hung up. She looked at Kevin's eating utensils, still on the table, snatched them up and threw them into the sink. They clanged as they ricocheted off the metal sides.

"Damn you," she said, then realized she wasn't sure who she was angry with. Was it Kevin, her mother, God, or herself?

◆

On a Saturday morning Nora ate brunch at the Holiday Inn with her mother. Their relationship had not changed much since high school. Back then she hadn't been sure what she wanted to do. After graduation her mother had suggested she go to secretarial school and see how she liked it. Nora had liked it just fine. When she finished, she landed a job with the university. Nora was still the dutiful daughter who accompanied her parents to church on Sundays and had lunch with her mother for lunch once a week, but lately she began feeling that she needed more space.

"How did Kevin like the Chicken Marbella?" her mother asked.

"Just fine." Nora picked up the menu. She knew her mother didn't really care if Kevin liked the chicken. She wasn't about to get into Kevin's hasty retreat. That would be too embarrassing. Or would it? Maybe she should level with her mother and let her know that it wasn't working out with Kevin. But she knew what her mother would say. God's plan, if he willed it, would come to pass. Besides, they didn't really discuss the vision anymore. It was like the elephant in the room.

Nora scanned the brunch special, then turned it over and studied the bar offerings. She had never ordered alcohol with her mother, but today she wanted to show her independence.

The waiter came over and Nora ordered the piña colada.

"Ma'am?"

Nora's mother smiled. "Just some grapefruit juice with ice for me."

When the waiter left, her mother continued to smile. "Well," she began, "you don't usually have alcohol before brunch."

There was the smile, thought Nora. The mother's smile—the smile that found it amusing that her twenty-four-year-old daughter was beginning to act like a grownup. But there was something else in the smile. The corners of her mother's mouth were raised unnaturally, like her lips were straining to lift the whole face. Nora knew what that smile meant. She was well aware of her father's struggle with the bottle.

"It's only a cocktail before brunch," she said.

The smile softened. "Of course dear, you're an adult now. I keep forgetting."

"You don't have to worry." Nora reached over the table to pat her mother's hand. "I feel in the mood for something different, that's all."

"He seemed like such a nice young man," her mother said.

"Oh." Nora stirred her drink with a straw. "I didn't have much of a chance to look at him."

"No, I mean Kevin, not the waiter." She laughed. "I'm so glad you had a chance to get to know him better before he left. Do you have any plans to write?"

Nora took a sip of the piña colada.

"Yes, Mother, we're going to write."

Nora's mother reached across the table and squeezed her arm. "You're a very lucky girl. Don't worry. God has a plan for you."

Nora smiled back. "Thanks, Mother, I hope He does."

———————◆———————

Two weeks after Kevin left for Ecuador, Nora started waking up in the middle of the night, then having trouble falling back to sleep. One morning she awoke with a dream still playing vividly in her mind.

She was at a high school dance feeling lost and alone when she spotted Kevin. She started walking toward him but he disappeared. Later, she found Kevin in a crowd of girls with dark complexions and colorful peasant dresses. The scene changed. Kevin was driving her car and her mother was in the back seat. They drove to an old house. Nora followed Kevin inside then lost him again. She awoke with a start feeling empty and reached out for Kevin.

The two exchanged letters, although not as often as she would have liked. He told her about the cool mountain climate and the difficulty of communicating in the local Indian dialect. She wrote back and told him how much she admired his dedication. He continued to appear in Nora's dreams, first as a friend but later as a lover who tempted her, and when she awoke, she was wet and wished she had a man lying next to her.

6

The Man of La Manacha

DR. THOMAS NEDERMAN WAS SITTING ON HIS BACK PORCH and had just finished reading a magazine article about Indiana Jones star Harrison Ford. *Funny how things happen*, he thought. Ford had become a carpenter to support his family because he wasn't making enough money playing bit parts in Hollywood. Then he built a cabinet for George Lucas, and just like that, he gets a contract. Nederman sighed. "Wish I'd had a lucky break like that when I was growing up."

Nederman put down the magazine, took a sip of beer and gazed at the brown sagebrush covered hill in back of his house. *What if, instead of pursuing the academic life, I had become an actor? If a carpenter can become a movie star why couldn't I?*

Suddenly he imagined himself in the middle of a Moroccan desert. George Lucas was making a movie about an archeologist who had stolen a 5000-year-old mummy and was trying to sell it to the Germans. Nederman was a famous actor hired to play the archeologist. Cameras, sound booms, scaffolding, and tents were crammed into a small area. The desert spread out like a huge ocean of sand in all directions. The cameramen were waiting for the signal.

"Action," shouted Lucas, wearing a floppy canvas hat.

Nederman looked up and squinted. A band of Bedouins were riding over the crest of the hill with their dark robes flying in the wind and the dust from the horses trailing behind them. They were coming to take the mummy. His character knew he couldn't fight them all, but hoped to use his cunning to convince them he didn't have it. He walked into the yard, coolly sizing them up. The one on the black stallion holding the huge scimitar stopped in front of him and dismounted. He had a well-trimmed black beard and a gold headband.

"Where are the artifacts?" he demanded. "They belong to our people. We know you have them and we will kill you unless you tell us."

"Well, that would be very unfortunate," said Nederman's character.

"It would be very unfortunate for you," sneered the bandit. "We will cut off your testicles and let you bleed to death in the desert."

"Well then, it would be very unfortunate for both of us," Nederman's character said with a grin. "I would die painfully and you would leave without your precious artifacts."

The bandit stared at him.

"Come, you must be thirsty after your long ride," said the archeologist, now in control. "Please accept my hospitality. Come in out of the sun and let me offer you some water. You can rest your horses next to the river. We will talk."

"CUT," yelled Lucas. He ran over to Nederman and clapped him on the back, "Great take. I think that's a wrap."

Nederman was shaken out of his reverie by a woman's voice.

"Tom, dinner's ready."

He snapped his head around. "Be there in a minute, honey." George Lucas would have to wait.

He took a last breath of the cool dry air and stepped inside. On the way to the dining room, he stopped to look at a framed photograph of himself dressed as the fifteenth century Spanish knight, Don Quixote. He took the picture from the bookshelf and rubbed some dust off. A proud looking young man with a dark beard and a metal helmet stared back at him. He smiled. The beard had remained for several years before he shaved it off at the request of a girlfriend. He slowly placed the picture back on the bookcase and smiled sadly. Anything seemed possible back then.

Dr. Nederman had met his wife when she was a student in one of his classes. They had run into each other at a watering hole near campus and soon started dating. When Ann became pregnant, Nederman had mixed feelings about becoming a father and hinted that Ann might want to consider an abortion. Ann, who was Catholic, wanted to get married. Nederman's career was on the line. It wouldn't look right for a single college professor to get his girlfriend pregnant, especially when he taught in the counseling department.

They were married in a simple ceremony in the campus chapel. Six months later, Jason was born. After Dr. Nederman made tenure, they bought their current home. Ann went back to school when Jason started kindergarten and received her Master's in Family Counseling. She worked part time with Dr. Nederman's colleague, but stopped when he left town. Ann settled into being a housewife, joined a gourmet cooking club, and put on thirty pounds.

Ann set a place for him at the dining room table and was in the kitchen putting the final touches on the salad.

"I was just thinking," he called to her as he sat down. "Do you remember that play I was in at the community theater, the one where I played Don Quixote?"

"You mean the musical, *The Man of La Manacha?*"

"Yes, yes, that was it."

"What about it?"

"I think I was pretty good. Sometimes I wish I had changed my major from psychology to theater." Ann had prepared her usual Sunday night meal, spaghetti and a Tuscan salad with pine nuts and dates.

"You know what?" said Dr. Nederman after Ann brought the salad. "I regret not becoming an actor. I think I had a real talent there. When I acted I felt like I was totally… free."

Ann sighed. Now he wanted to be an actor. Last week it was a jet pilot. She knew he was going through a mid-life crisis but wasn't quite sure how to handle him. In the past, she had mentioned to him the possibility that he was going through a change of life. The first time he said he was too young for a mid-life crisis. He was only 52-years old and felt fine. He just wanted to develop some latent talent. The second time she brought it up was when he wanted to buy a motorcycle. She convinced him to buy a sports car instead

"What's wrong with being a college professor?" she said, dishing up some spaghetti on her plate, and then handing the bowl to her husband. "It's a good living and you get your summers off. Maybe you could get involved with The Pocatello Players, do some summer stock."

Dr. Nederman took the bowl of spaghetti and served himself with the tongs. Ann had brought up the summer stock idea before. At first it seemed like a good idea, but the more he thought about it the less he liked it.

"I'm not talking about summer stock," he said. "It's just that I'm getting bored with the academic life. Everything is so predictable. Yesterday I was at a faculty meeting and got this *deja vu* feeling. It's happening more and more. I've done it, been there." He reached for the spaghetti sauce and knocked over a glass of beer.

"Oh, oh," said Ann. "I'll get a sponge." She jumped up and ran into the kitchen. "I'll bet you didn't predict that," she called back jokingly. When she returned he was staring at the ever expanding stain on the table cloth. She patted it with a sponge.

"You just like the image of being married to a college professor," he said with a bit of sarcasm. He poured some more beer into his glass. "Sure, we've got lots of material stuff," he said, holding out his hands and looking around the room. "But it's only stuff. What are we going to do with it? Sit around here looking at it for the rest of our lives?"

Ann rolled her eyes. They sat in silence while Nederman twirled the spaghetti on his fork. The academic womb did provide financial security, he thought, and he couldn't fault her for that. But she had lost her sense of adventure. He remembered that before they were married they would have sex behind the bushes on campus when the moon was full. The risk of getting caught intensified the erotic experience. Now they usually had sex in the evening, sandwiched in between computer work and being so tired that sleep was all that mattered.

"Honey," began Ann, "we've worked hard for 'this stuff' and now it's our time in life to enjoy it. At least I plan to enjoy it." She looked at her husband, hoping for a reply, but he was just staring at the table.

An awful feeling came over Nederman. Something was sucking the life out of him. His training told him that he was going through a midlife crisis. He had counseled other men who had gone through it. He would tell them it was a normal part of growing older. They were changing physically and their self-concept would have to change. He would tell them that to live life is to feel inferior sometimes. The trick was to not act inferior. They could reshape their own personalities and destinies. Take risks. Reframe their lives.

Yet here he was, wrapping spaghetti noodles around a fork just like his life was being wrapped tightly around a concept; Dr. Nederman, college professor, therapist, husband, fixer of other people, and writer of academic papers. He took a breath and looked around. So this is what his life had become—a good job with summers off. He closed his eyes. *Maybe it will pass. Don't try to control it.* Suddenly he realized that the "it" wasn't really an "it." The "it" was his self.

He looked up from the table. Ann was smiling at him.

"I know, I know," he said. "Just hear me out. Ever since I was a young man I've wanted to make something of myself. My parents didn't want me to work in their bakery for the rest of my life and neither did I. Sure; I helped with the family business. But they depended on me. I would get up at 4 a.m., load the truck and then deliver bread and rolls before going to school. Sometimes I could barely stay awake in class, but I studied hard and managed to get a scholarship to the University of Utah. I majored in psychology and... here I am. End of story." He threw up his hands.

"You have done very well for yourself," said Ann. "You should be proud." She stood up and began clearing the table. "Do you want some dessert?" she asked. "I could make some strawberry short cake."

"Ah, no, that's okay, honey. I think I'll go outside for a while."

He pushed the back chair and wandered out to the porch. The sun was setting. The place from where the desert nomads had come was now just a low hill scattered with wilted cottonwoods and sagebrush barely visible in the fading light.

When Dr. Nederman arrived at the office Monday morning Nora was already sitting at her desk sorting through graduate school applications.

"Good morning, Dr. Nederman," said Nora.

"Good morning, Nora." He caught a wisp of a sweet fragrance with a tinge of lemon. "Mmmm...something smells very..." *He was going to say sexy, but he stopped himself,* "good."

"Oh, thank you. It's something new I'm trying called *Angel Fire*." Nora blushed.

"Good choice."

"I finished the conference schedules. They're on your desk."

"Thank you, I hope you didn't have to stay late."

Should I tell him? thought Nora. "Oh, not really," she said, rubbing her neck.

"Strain your neck?"

"Oh, it'll be all right," said Nora. "When I woke up it was bothering me a little. Just lying in the wrong position, I guess."

"If you need a neck rub, I'm the guy to help." He watched as she sat up straight and rolled her head in a slow circle, the line of her breasts standing out beneath her tight red sweater.

A neck massage would feel good, but would it be appropriate? Nora smiled, "No that's very sweet of you but I just have to get up and walk around a little." She enjoyed working with Dr. Nederman, and once they even had lunch together at the student union. He had told her a funny story about a chicken on his farmette that had become a pet because of its unusual antics. They laughed and laughed about that one. She liked his sense of humor and warmth.

Dr. Nederman went into his office and turned the lights on. His desk was in a corner to the right in front of a long shelf jammed with books. On the left side of the room was a leather armchair he used for counseling. Beside the armchair was a silver floor lamp with a saucer shaped shade. On the wall beside the chair were framed photographs of Sigmund Freud with a cigar in his hand, a bearded Fritz Pearls, and Alfred Adler dressed in a three piece suit. He sat down and looked at a draft of the conference schedule Nora had placed on his desk. *Angel Fire.* He could still smell it.

He made a few corrections on the schedule and called Nora into his office.

"Have a seat."

Nora pulled up a chair.

"No, over there," said Dr. Nederman, pointing to the armchair. "I can't have my secretary in pain all day with a stiff neck."

Nora hesitated, then sat down.

Nederman got up and walked over to her chair. "Just relax. I give therapeutic massages all the time."

Nora smiled. "All right… I guess it's tighter than I thought."

7

18-214

ZACK VOLUNTEERED TO HELP TRANSPORT BILLY BUTTS, a patient who had assaulted a police officer, to a court hearing in Northern Idaho. Zack thought it would be a good way to see the mountains and get paid for it at the same time. They left Blackfoot in the security truck at 5 a.m. Tom, one of the older security officers, drove and Zack rode shotgun. Tom was an ex-sheriff's deputy. He wore a brown Stetson with a silver Navajo bola and had a well-trimmed grey mustache. Billy, his cuffs unshackled and wearing an old army fatigue jacket, rode in the back seat behind a security mesh.

After they hit on the Interstate, Tom popped open a window, lit a cigarette and turned to Zack. "Just wondering, how'd you happened to get a job at the State Hospital?"

Zack poured a cup of coffee from the thermos and offered it to Tom, then poured himself a cup. "Every time I applied for a mental health job in Wisconsin there were about a hundred people ahead of me. I was tired of waiting. Besides, I always wanted to live out West."

"So, how come you wanted to work in mental health?"

Zack took a sip of coffee. "Is there something wrong with that?"

"Not a thing, I just wonder why people go into the field. I started out as a deputy in Arco, but transferred to the State Hospital because I had a family to take care of and needed the benefits."

Zack leaned back against the door. He took another drag off his cigarette and blew the smoke out of the opening at the top of his window. "It's about the only job you can find with a psychology degree. Besides, maybe I can help someone."

"Maybe you can," said Tom with a smile. "God knows there sure are a lot of people who need help in this world. Trouble is, getting them to let you help. Take Billy back there, for example. He gets disability payments from the feds for having a nervous breakdown in the service. Whenever he gets committed, the state can't touch the disability because it's always an involuntary commitment. He has a nice little nest egg built up when he gets out. This last time he came here from the Kootenai County Jail after he ransacked his parent's house." Tom glanced over at Zack. "Yep, sure are a lot of people who need help."

Zack thought about friends who were addicted to drugs and an old girlfriend who had suffered from depression. He wasn't able to help them. He pictured the vacant stares of the residents of the half-way house where he used to work. They never changed. *Hell, I can't even help myself sometimes.*

They drove north toward Salmon, across the flat, dry Snake River Valley where small patches of black volcanic soil supported colonies of squat, greenish-grey sagebrush scattered amidst ancient lava flows. Just before sunrise, the dark silhouettes of the Teton Mountains appeared in the east like sentinels against the red dawn. When they stopped for breakfast in Salmon, they woke Billy and cuffed him.

The diner had a small counter and one row of booths along the opposite wall.

A young waitress with dark hair pulled into a bun came over to their booth glanced at Billy, then looked down at her order pad. "What can I get for you gentlemen."

While they were waiting for their coffee, Billy recounted the series of events that led to his arrest. He was having problems during his first day of classes at the university and became upset when he couldn't see his counselor. He yelled at the secretary then walked downtown to complain to his old Marine recruiting sergeant. The sergeant was about to go home and didn't have time to talk. When Billy refused to leave, the sergeant contacted the university's counseling office.

They advised him to call the campus security. When they arrived, Billy still refused to leave, so they obtained backup. Billy was booked into the county jail. He gave a blow by blow description of the scuffle he had with a jailer as he was being booked. "That old sonovabitch didn't know what hit him." When no one responded, Billy continued. "I kicked the old bastard in the nuts."

"Why'd you do that?" asked Zack.

"The old fucker was trying to feel me up and told me to take off my pants. Man, I kicked him right in the balls. He dropped like a sack of shit. 'Don't fuck with me,' I told him. 'Nobody fucks with me.'"

Zack shrugged and let it drop. He knew better than to get into a moral argument with a sociopath.

"Hey, Zack," said Billy when the coffee came. "Could you be so kind as to take these cuffs off, so I can drink my coffee?"

Zack exchanged smiles with Tom. "Sorry, Billy, you'll have to do the best you can." He took a drag off of his cigarette. "Regulations."

"What the fuck. You can't make an exception?"

"Now, Billy, you know that if we make an exception in your case we'll have to make an exception in everyone's case and pretty soon there won't be no rules at all for no one," said Tom, giving Zack a wink.

Billy began trying to drink with both hands, but the short chain between his wrist cuffs and his belt was barely long enough and he spilled some coffee on his lap.

"Good Lord, look at you," said Tom, shaking his head. He

reached down to his belt and pulled out a set of keys on the end of a retractable chain.

He unlocked one cuff. "I guess I'm going to have to make an exception for you after all. Here," he said, handing Billy a napkin. "Wipe yourself off. We just can't take you nowhere, now, can we?" When they finished breakfast Tom re-cuffed Billy.

From Salmon, they headed into Montana and reached Missoula by midday, then drove west, across the Bitterroot Range and back into Idaho.

It was a long downhill drive west toward Coeur d 'Alene with many switchbacks and blind curves. As they passed rock outcroppings, Tom told them of their differing mineral contents. He was going to retire soon and intended to work an abandoned gold mine he had recently purchased. He said the reddish rocks were full of iron ore, the yellow rocks contained sulfur, and the rocks with a green tinge carried copper deposits. The mountains were honeycombed with working mines and small isolated towns with names like Smelterville, Silverton, Kellogg, and Wallace. Railroad tracks paralleled the road, and every now and then, they would see a crude wooden and tin chute jutting from the side of a hill.

When they reached Orofino, they took Billy to the jail and waited while he was booked. Billy sat at a desk across from a very large deputy.

"How you doing there, Mr. Deputy," Billy said cheerfully. "I grew up in this town, so I want you to know that I have a lot of friends here. I've been away for a while but after the judge lets me out, I'll stop in and see you boys from time to time." Billy snickered. "Do you play five card monty?"

The deputy pointed a finger at Billy. "You, shut up."

Zack and Tom exchanged grins.

That evening, Zack walked around Orofino. The small town was nestled between two mountains in a little valley with the Orofino River meandering through it. Zack had checked the elevation on the map and noticed that it was only 2,000 feet. The moist evening air held the sweet scent of evergreens and reminded him of northern Wisconsin.

The next morning, they drove to the courthouse, which was attached to the jail. While walking down the old dimly lit hallway to the courtroom, Zack stopped to squint at ancient photographs of former judges, some with handlebar mustaches and long beards.

As he approached the courtroom, Zack noticed a tall man wearing blue jeans and a cowboy hat leaning against a wall at the end of the corridor.

"Howdy, my name is Jeff Walker," he said, extending his hand. "I'm a psychologist at State Hospital South."

"I haven't seen you before," said Tom. "You must be new."

"I moved here about four months ago from back East."

"Where were you living?" Zack asked.

"New York."

Zack looked down at the man's cowboy boots, then up to his white Stetson hat. "I see you haven't had any trouble fitting in," he said with a broad grin.

"This is how I dressed back in New York City, too. People used to laugh at me behind my back. No one laughs at me here."

"Welcome to Idaho," said Tom.

"Are you going to testify?" Zack asked.

"Yes. I examined Billy and he seems like he's a troubled, but basically good, fellow."

Zack bit his tongue.

A uniformed officer came down the hall and opened the courtroom doors.   They entered a small chamber with three rows of spectator seats and sat down. Billy's attorney, a short man with a rumpled suit and a battered briefcase, came in and sat down at a table then everyone stood again as the judge entered, carrying a large file. He sat down, put on a pair of gold wire rimmed glasses, and began leafing through the file. He looked too young, Zack thought, to be a judge. He wore his dark hair slightly over his ears and he had a wispy mustache. After about a minute, he looked up and scanned the room.

"Is the defendant, Billy Butts, in the room?" he asked.

"Ah, no sir," said Billy's lawyer. "He's still in the jail."

"Bring him in."

"Yes sir," said the bailiff.

He left the room and returned with Billy, who shuffled into the courtroom with leg irons and a grey jumpsuit.

After he sat down, the judge addressed Billy. "It says here that you are currently in the custody of the Department of Health and Welfare on an 18-214, which means you are pleading not guilty to assault by reason of insanity. Is that right?"

Billy looked up and nodded.

"Please speak up so the clerk can record your response."

"Yes sir. That's what I'm pleading."

"It also says that you were discharged from the state hospital but have violated your conditions of release. You assaulted a police officer at the Bannock County Sheriff's Office while being booked on a misdemeanor trespassing charge." The judge turned to Billy's lawyer. "Mr. Brown, does your client understand the charges?"

"Yes sir," he said, rising half-way. "He does."

The judge glanced at another piece of paper then looked around the room. "Is Mr. Walker in the courtroom?"

"Yes sir, I am."

"Have you had a chance to examine Mr. Butts?"

"Yes, I have, Your Honor."

"Well then, come forward, and the clerk will get you sworn in."

The cowboy-psychologist took the stand and stated his name and credentials. Mr. Brown asked him for his evaluation of Billy.

"I met with Mr. Butts last night at the jail," Mr. Walker began. "This young man has had a very long and troubled history of incarceration in several state and county facilities due to his long battle with mental illness after he was discharged from the United States Marine Corps. At the time of his arrest, it seems that Mr. Butts was suffering from an acute psychotic episode."

"Acute psychotic episode," repeated Mr. Brown, slowly enunciating each word. "Given his state of mind at the time, would you say that Mr. Butts could appreciate the seriousness of his actions?"

"No. I don't think that he could, given the nature of the diagnosis."

Billy's lawyer turned to the judge and shrugged. "I have no more questions, your Honor."

The judge dismissed Walker and called Dr. Able to the stand. Able was the doctor who advised the Marine recruiter to call the police. With his bald head, goatee, and three-piece suit, he precisely fit the stereotype of a psychiatrist.

He waited as Billy and his lawyer conferred in hushed voices. Finally Mr. Brown stood up and approached Dr. Able.

"Dr. Able, are you the one who advised Sgt. Torres to

call the police?"

"Yes I did."

"Well, sir, I want to set the scene for you." Mr. Brown stepped back and made a frame with his hands. "Mr. Butts has just been released from six months in a mental hospital. He's extremely apprehensive about going to college, but has summoned up the courage to give it a try, to improve his life and become a productive citizen. He makes an appointment with a counselor who is supposed to help guide him through the first confusing weeks but the counselor is too busy to see him. So he goes to the person who has helped him in the past, Sgt. Torres, his old Marine recruiter. Couldn't it have been that Mr. Butts was just trying to confide in Sgt. Torres, man to man?"

"I'm sure he was trying to get some help, but the way Sgt. Torres described it to me, Mr. Butts was out of control. I thought the police would be better equipped to deal with these situations than the sergeant," said Able in a calm and even tone.

"Is it possible that you may have misinterpreted what the sergeant said and erroneously recommended that he call the police?" Mr. Brown asked.

"Of course there is always that possibility, but given the nature of the incident, I thought it was prudent to err on the side of caution."

"Yes indeed, err on the side of caution, well ahh..." Mr. Brown turned to the judge. "That's all I have to say."

Dr. Able stepped down. Several others testified, including the jailer who was kicked. Billy watched the proceedings, alternatively fidgeting with his beard and burying his face on the table.

Finally, Billy's lawyer called on him to testify. He shuffled toward the bench and stepped up into the witness stand, his chains making loud dragging noises on the wooden steps. Billy's thin frame was dwarfed by the large mahogany chair. The bailiff swore him in and his lawyer asked him to tell the judge his version of what happened.

"Look," Billy began. "I know I made a mistake. I'm sorry for what I did, but at the time I was feeling really scared." He lowered his head and looked upward in desperation. "I waited and waited to talk with a counselor but no one wanted to see me. I could feel the frustration building up, so I went to see the only friend I had left, Sgt. Torres. I tried to keep things under control, but I suddenly felt like a dam was breaking. People were grabbing at me and trying to hurt me. I had to protect myself." Billy ran his fingers through his hair. "I'm sorry," he said, his voice quivering, "but I just wanted to talk to someone."

Billy bit his lip and looked away.

"Do you want to further question your client?" asked the judge.

"No your honor."

"Then you may step down."

After a 30-minute recess, the judge spoke directly to Billy. "I think you are a very intelligent young man, but since you have violated almost every condition of your release I have no option other than to remand you to the custody of the state. I would be glad to review your case in six months." He pounded his gavel. "Good luck."

Before they loaded Billy into the truck the following morning, Zack noticed that he had a smug grin on his face. Suddenly, Zack felt a surge of anger and wanted to slap the grin off Billy's face.

"You're pretty slick, aren't you?" Zack, tried to control himself.

"What do you mean?"

"Oh I think you know. You manipulated Dr. Able into giving you a diagnosis, retaining your disability payments, then you convinced the judge that you are reasonably sane, opening the way for a future release."

"I've still got to put up with you assholes," said Billy with a nervous laugh.

"That's just the way things should be, "said Tom, climbing into the driver's seat. "We're all just making tons of money putting up with each other."

Zack took a deep breath and relaxed. He was glad they were with Tom. The old cowboy had a way of taking the edge off a confrontation.

8

The Ice Queen

NOW THAT ZACK WAS MAKING MONEY AGAIN, he moved twenty-five miles south to Pocatello and signed up for an evening course in psychology at Idaho State University. He had decided to obtain a master's degree in counseling which would qualify him to work as a psychologist.

The sun was just setting as he pulled the Starchief into a campus parking lot and checked his watch. "Gotta hurry, shit, first day of class and I'm already going to be late."

He grabbed his notebook and ran toward the large, four-story psychology building.

Now, where's the classroom? He had jotted it down, but where? He stopped and began flipping through his notebook. He saw the number "154." *That must be it.* Once inside, he located the small room at the end of a long hallway and took a seat. He looked around. There was a man in his thirties with a business suit and two young women with skirts and pumps. Behind them, three young men wearing blue work shirts and jeans slumped at their desks. A man with a gray beard and long hair looked at Zack but turned away when their eyes met. Zack smiled. "Bunch of working stiffs," he muttered.

The professor, an attractive middle-aged woman with dark hair, wrote on the chalk board: "Survey of Current Psychotherapies 201. Linda Blackburn Ph.D."

She looked at her watch and turned to the class.

"Is everyone here signed up for 201?" She slowly looked around the room then glanced down at the podium and began calling the role. "Welcome to the course," she said when she was finished. "We'll be using Corsini's textbook because..."

That was the last clear memory Zack had of the first lecture because his attention was diverted by a young woman entering the room. She had a petite figure and wore designer jeans and black high-heeled shoes. She moved quickly, looking at no one. Zack's eyes tracked her as she moved to the back of the room and sat down.

"And your name is..." asked Blackburn?

"Nora," said the young woman. "Nora Fairchild."

"Welcome to 201," said the professor with a smile.

Nora slipped off her purse and took out a small notebook.

The smell of elegant perfume had trailed her and drifted over to Zack's side of the room. He inhaled deeply. *What was it?* The odor reminded him of the elegant cocktail parties his parents used to throw. The young woman had well-manicured frosted nails and was wearing a tight, glittering sweater that accented her large breasts. Her short blond hair was impeccably coifed. Zack glanced at her and smiled, but she appeared not to notice.

Zack looked back at Professor Blackburn, catching fragments of her lecture. "... and as we go through the different therapies I want you to keep in mind that... people often react to the therapist in ways that are... When you finish with this course I hope you have a..."

Zack couldn't keep his eyes off Nora and wondered what was behind her cold beauty. Was she a high class hooker? If she was, Zack figured he might as well forget becoming involved. On the other hand, maybe she was a woman who was trapped inside a gorgeous façade just waiting for her prince charming to set her free.

When class was over, she left quickly. As she disappeared in the hallway, Zack knew what he wanted to get out of the course. He had been without a woman for too long. He wanted the Ice Queen.

Dr. Nederman gently moved his fingers down the sides of Nora's neck applying just the right amount of pressure to locate problem areas.

"You feel tight," he said.

"Yes, I woke up this morning again with a kink in my neck."

Nora had grown accustomed to Dr. Nederman giving her neck

rubs. As soon as she felt his gentle hands on her neck, she began to relax. After the third session he had insisted she call him Tom. Nora would not normally have permitted her boss to touch her like that, but this was different, she thought. Dr. Nederman was a therapist.

"How is it going with the new apartment," he asked.

"I had to pay two months' rent in advance, put down a security deposit and now I need furniture. So, outside of being broke, I guess I'm okay," Nora grinned.

"I received a note from admin the other day, and you are up for a pay raise."

"Yes, I saw an email the other day," said Nora rolling her neck. "I could sure use it now."

"Oh, don't worry. I plan to give you a glowing recommendation. I feel… I hope you don't take this the wrong way… but I feel like we have a special relationship. We work well together and I enjoy helping you relax. You really keep me in practice."

"Thank you Doctor… I mean Tom… that means a lot to me."

Nora noticed the smell of his cologne as he moved his face closer in. Dr. Nederman moved his hands over her shoulders and down her arms. She stiffened. *Maybe I shouldn't do this.* He lifted her elbows then dropped them.

"A little muscle tension here," he said. "Just relax." He lifted them up again and watched as she let them flop to her sides. "That's better. You're doing very well."

"That feels wonderful, Doctor... I mean Tom."

"You deserve it. You're the best secretary I've ever had. I don't know what I'd do without you."

Nora felt a glow come over her. She patted Dr. Nederman's hand and said, "Thank you."

Her eyes were closed when Dr. Nederman brushed his hand quickly across her breast.

"Excuse me."

"That's okay." Nora appreciated how considerate he was. Once, when he drove her home from work, she almost fell into his lap as they turned a corner a little too quickly. He apologized for that, too.

"Let me take a look at your shoulders," he said, moving to a chair in front of her. "I want to make sure they are in alignment."

When she opened her eyes, Dr.Nederman had a bashful, puppy dog look on his face. Nora leaned forward and gave him a quick kiss on the cheek. He opened his eyes wide and smiled, then both of them giggled.

Slowly and gently, he moved his hands down Nora's arms again then began caressing the edge of her breasts.

Nora sat up as Nederman let his hands slip to his sides.

"Is something wrong?"

Nora wanted him to like her, to think she was special, yet she didn't want to be taken advantage of.

"I like getting a massage from you but I…"

"I know you're enjoying this." Nederman's voice grew firmer. He reached around her back and unclipped her bra.

"This form of massage has been used in Indonesia for years. Trust me. It will relieve all your tension." He moved behind her, reached around and began rubbing her nipples. She felt a rush of passion mixed with foreboding.

She tried to get up, but Dr. Nederman eased her back.

Then, for a moment Nora thought it might be all right. He sounded so sure of himself. The expert with honorary degrees from prestigious institutions of higher learning plastered to his walls. Before she knew it, she had let him go too far.

He removed his slacks and pulled her over to the futon wasting no time in forever transforming the nature of their relationship. When they finished, he pulled a comforter over them and cuddled up to Nora.

She jerked away.

"What's wrong?"

"I…I… " Nora turned away.

"You sounded like you enjoyed it." When Nora didn't reply, Dr.

Nederman whispered, "Don't worry. This can be our little secret." He moved a curl from in front of her eyes and kissed her forehead.

"I have to go now," she said, grabbing the comforter as she tried to push herself off the futon.

Nederman stood up and gave her his hand. "You can use the bathroom to get dressed."

Nora gathered up her clothes. After she pulled her slacks on and tucked in her blouse, she looked at herself in the mirror and began to cry. Curls stood out from her hair at all angles and her tears mixed with mascara, forming dark lines down her cheeks. She took a deep breath, wiped her eyes with toilet paper and still couldn't believe what just happened.

9

7&7 and a Pack of Smokes

TWO WEEKS INTO HIS PSYCHOLOGY CLASS, Zack finished his night shift at the state hospital and drove home to Pocatello. The sun was bright and helped him stay awake. A half hour later he pulled up to his apartment in an older two-flat located a half block from the Union Pacific Railroad tracks. He fed Otis then watched TV until he became tired and went to bed. He was awakened by the ringing of his telephone. He picked up the receiver.

"Hey, Zack, how's it going?" said a woman with a gravelly voice. It sounded familiar.

"Who is this?"

"Hey man, its Sonya, how the hell you doing?"

The name slowly floated into his consciousness. Perhaps he was dreaming.

"Hello Zack, are you there?"

"Sonya?"

"Yeah, man, this is Sonya. How the hell are you?"

Otis jumped on the bed and began pawing Zack's neck. Zack glanced over at the clock. It was 2 p.m. He wasn't dreaming.

He pushed Otis away and sat up. "I'm okay, been working the night shift."

"Oh, hey man, I didn't mean to wake you up. I'll call back later if you want. I just wanted to see if you were still in town. I got your number from information, but if you want to sleep, I can call you back."

Zack wiped his eyes. *What is Sonya doing in Pocatello?* He had thought about calling her in Montpelier, but decided against it. He had a new job and was trying to move on with his life. Yet, he wanted to know what she was up to. He was wide awake now.

"No, that's okay. Where are you staying?"

"I'm driving a little camper and saw a campground on the way in today, really nice with a little stream flowing through it and a bar right next door."

"What's the name of the bar?"

"The Come Back Inn."

"I have some errands to run. I'll meet you there around, how about four o'clock."

"Well, all right," said Sonya. "How's Otis?"

"Otis is good. Talk to you later."

Zack fixed a pot of coffee then walked to the grocery store for a pack of cigarettes. The bright sun helped him reset his body clock.

The Come Back Inn was a little bar on the edge of town. It was owned by an ex-biker who had pictures of Harleys and motorcycle mamas all over the walls. He smiled and shook his head: just the place for Sonya. When he walked in, the juke box was playing a Willy Nelson song. The smell of French fries filled the air. Zack ordered a beer and lit a cigarette. At the end of the bar, two cowboys were shaking dice in a leather cup then slapping it on the bar. No one was on the pool table; Zack decided to shoot a rack, when the door swung open. In walked Sonya. She was wearing sunglasses, high-heeled boots, and carried a fringed buckskin purse on her shoulder. Her poofed-up red hair gave her extra stature.

"Well, look what the cat just dragged in," said Zack with a grin.

Sonya whipped off her glasses. "Hey, Zack," she said. When she came closer, Zack noticed the top buttons of her shirt were undone, revealing a generous view of her cleavage. "How the fuck are you?" She gave him a hug.

"Not bad," said Zack. She felt good and smelled good and was wearing the same brand of perfume she wore the last time they had sex. He felt himself stirring, but he knew Sonya probably wanted more than just a roll in the hay.

He put his arm around her and they walked over to the bar. The two cowboys stopped their game of dice long enough to give her the once over.

The bartender, an old man with a white mustache, walked over.

"Give the lady a 7&7," said Zack.

When the drinks came, they found a table and Sonya told Zack about the last few months. She had become involved with a small group of cocaine traffickers who were bringing the drugs up from Mexico, but was busted and became a DEA informant.

"Zack, I didn't want to rat on anyone, but what could I do?" she said in a loud whisper.

Zack rolled his eyes. "What else could you do?"

He bought her another drink

"How about a game of pool?" said Sonya. "We'll play for drinks." She popped two quarters into the slot on the side of the pool table and racked up the balls.

"Go ahead and break," she said.

Zack managed to knock a striped ball into a pocket but missed his next shot. Sonya ran the next four balls, the last one a thin bank into the side pocket.

"Oooooo...I don't believe I made that one," she cooed. She missed her next shot. As Zack was about to shoot, a cowboy put two quarters on the edge of the pool table, then returned to his seat.

Zack knew the routine. Sonya would strut her stuff for a while, throwing her hair back and laughing until some guy would challenge her. She'd lose a couple games then flash him a smile and get him to put up some money. The more they lost, the more they drank, and the more they drank the more she'd win. Around bar time, she would go to the ladies room then slip out a side door.

The more Zack drank, the better Sonya looked to him with her long cowgirl legs and teased up red hair. After she missed a shot, he put his arm around her and gave her a pat on the ass.

"Hey there, honky-tonk woman. You better watch out. Your luck might be changing." He missed the next shot and Sonya ran the table on him.

One of the cowboys from the bar sauntered over and pushed two quarters in the coin slot and pulled it out. The balls clacked together as they rolled down into reservoir. He squatted down, removed the balls and set them in the rack. Sonya broke but didn't get any balls in. The cowboy circled the table then shot right into a cluster, inadvertently sinking the eight ball.

"Shit," he said and shook his head, then went back to playing dice with his friend. Zack paid for the next game and Sonya broke. She was just lining up a shot when three men walked in. Two of them wore cowboy hats and the other a baseball cap. As she glanced up at them, her eyes widened and her mouth opened slightly. She hit the cue-ball low, causing it to fly off the table and bounce along on the floor until it came to rest at the foot of the one with the baseball cap. He picked it up and slowly handed it to Sonya.

He turned to the other two men and smiled. "Well, look who's here."

"Don't you remember us?" said one of them wearing a beat-up cowboy hat. He towered over the others and had a goatee.

Sonya accepted the ball and placed it on the table. "Oh, yeah, how are you boys doing?" she said nonchalantly.

"We're doing all right," said the tall one. "Can't say the same for Ronnie and James though, can I boys?" He gave them a tense smile.

Zack lined up a shot. He had a feeling that something bad was going to happen. *Who are these guys? What is it she said earlier, something about having ratted on someone?* He felt a knot in his stomach. He took a breath, slowly let the air out and shot. He sank a ball in the corner pocket and walked around to the end of the table, where the three men were standing.

"Excuse me, fellows," he said. They moved but not much.

"I don't know if I ever seen this one," said the man in the baseball cap. He had his hair woven in a long pigtail in the back and had a chipped tooth.

Zack turned to Sonya. "Why don't you introduce me to your friends?"

She pointed to the man in the baseball cap. "That's Toker and that big guy is Charlie P. And that's Jeremiah," she said, pointing to the clean shaven one who looked to be the youngest.

"Howdy, I'm Zack."

Charlie P. ignored Zack and looked at Sonya. "Ain't you going to ask us about Ronnie and James?"

Sonya still had the smile on her face but it was becoming strained. "What about them?"

"They're in jail."

"I'm sorry to hear that," said Sonya coolly. Zack studied the pool balls with a feigned intensity. He glanced at the three mangy men out of the corner of his eye. They were quietly watching Sonya as she chalked her cue, twisting the stick back and forth until blue dust began pouring from the cube.

"Yeah, we're sorry, too," said Toker. "We're real sorry."

"Let's get us something to drink," said Charlie P. They found a table on the other side of the room and sat down, just out of earshot of Sonya and Zack, but still clearly in their view—like jackals observing their prey.

Zack moved to the other side of the table. "You want to tell me what this is all about?"

The pool table was in a little room off the main bar. Sonya moved to the end of the room, out of sight of the three men.

"I met this guy at the bar where I worked," Sonya began in a loud whisper. "We did a little blow. He seemed okay until one day he flashed his badge." Her eyes widened and she lowered her voice. "Zack, he was with the fucking DEA… the fucking DEA. I couldn't believe it."

Zack sank a ball in the corner. "That's funny," he said. "You were always such a fine judge of character."

Sonya didn't take the bait. "He said he needed some information on a drug operation." She downed her 7&7 and lit another cigarette.

Zack thought of leaving, but that wouldn't be good for Sonya. They'd probably hustle her outside, never to be seen again. She was a pain in the ass, but he wasn't about to abandon her.

"So who are Ronnie and James?"

"Toker's brothers," said Sonya. She blew some smoke into the air. "I used to work with them on the seismo crew. Ronnie slipped dynamite in the holes that James dug. They were both a couple of cokeheads. There was nothing to do except bust your ass all day humping cord up and down the mountains. Everyone had too much money to spend and not enough drugs. Anyway, one day some coke dealers from back east stopped into the bar looking to sell a large amount of product. They offered me a cut of the action. I figured I could finally get some money together and blow out of that shit hole, Zack. You know what I mean?"

Zack stared at Sonya, then looked away. "So you set up a deal."

"The DEA gave me $500, a truck, and I was out of there," said

Sonya. "Hey Zack, could you get me another 7&7 and a pack of smokes? I left my money in the truck."

Zack bought some more drinks and a pack of cigarettes at the bar then returned to the pool table. A couple of aging cowgirls with heavy makeup and tight jeans came in, took seats at the bar and began making flirtatious glances at Sonya's former co-workers.

"Here," he said, handing Sonya her drink. He looked toward the bar. "I don't think they'll try anything in here but I'm not staying here all day." Zack took a swig of beer. "Maybe we should make a run for it."

"I don't know. They'll probably come after us."

"Yeah, I know," said Zack. "But I have a plan. We'll split up."

"Why do we have to do that?" asked Sonya. "I'm gonna need a place to hole up. Why don't I meet you at your place?"

"Too risky," said Zack. He was thinking hard. "You'd better get as far away from here as possible. Why not head back to Wisconsin?"

"Wisconsin? There's nothing for me in Wisconsin."

"There's nothing for you here either."

Sonya looked confused. "I… I… thought we were buds, Zack."

Zack leaned across the table. "I know but things have changed. I have a good job now and I'm going back to school. I'm trying to start a new life here. It looks like we're taking two different paths."

Sonya hesitated for a moment. "So, you think you're too good for me, is that it? Just wait. Next time you need a friend, don't come crawling back. Fuck you, Zack." She grabbed her purse.

"Where are you going?"

"I'm leaving."

She walked toward the door with her pool stick. Charlie P. looked up.

"Where do you think you're going?"

Sonya kept walking toward the door. When Charlie P. tried to block her, she jammed the tip of the pool stick into his crotch. He let out a painful cry and fell to the floor. Sonya pushed open the door but Toker grabbed her from behind.

"Hey bitch, not so fast." He threw her across the room.

Zack threw a pool ball at Toker, catching him in the back of his head. Toker fell forward onto the table where the two aging cowgirls were seated. They screamed and tried to push him off.

Sonya brushed herself off and ran toward the door. Charlie P. was trying to get up, but Sonya kneed him in the face. He went down again.

Jeremiah, who was watching from the back of his booth, tried to stand, but Zack pushed him back. "Stay put."

Sonya was already out the door when the two aging cowgirls finally managed to slide Toker off their table. He staggered backwards and began rubbing his head. Charlie P. pulled himself up on a table.

The bartender grabbed the phone as Zack ran out the door. Sonya had already climbed into her camper, jammed it into reverse and was turning around.

"Turn left and head for town," he yelled to Sonya. "Just follow the signs for the interstate."

Sonya gunned her engine, gave Zack the finger, and screeched out, sending a plume of red dust into the air.

Zack jumped into the Starchief and waited. When Charlie P. and his friends came stumbling out, he floored the accelerator and headed in the opposite direction Sonya had taken. As he squealed around a curve he saw two squad cars approaching with their sirens wailing and lights flashing. He slowed down and tried to light a cigarette but his hands were shaking. He put the lighter away as the police cars passed. His heart was racing. When he got home, he sat in his car for a long time. After the shaking subsided, he managed to light the cigarette. He took a deep drag and slumped against the steering wheel. "Too close," he muttered. "Too close."

10

Predator

REBECCA FAIRCHILD ANTICIPATED something, but she wasn't sure what it was.

The feeling grew stronger as she drove to the post office to mail a package of cookies to her niece in Salt Lake City. She checked the rearview mirror to see if anyone was following her. When she left the post office, she was especially careful to look both ways before entering the stream of traffic. *Was Nora in danger?*

Rebecca's father, a minister, had taught her that if she wanted the Lord to hear her prayers, she had to be brave enough to talk to Him as if He was standing right in front of her. He called it fearlessness, a combination of faith and devotion.

"What are you trying to tell me, Lord?" she asked.

Suddenly she saw a brightly lit mannequin wearing a wedding dress in a shop window. Its arm was raised and its index finger was pointing at her. Her heart quickened. Rebecca swerved her car into the parking lot and walked into the shop.

"Excuse me," she said to the clerk, a heavy set young woman with straight black hair and glasses.

"Yes, ma'am."

"I was just driving by and I couldn't help noticing that taffeta wedding gown in your window."

The clerk walked toward the mannequin. "Oh, yes, you mean the one with the bridal veil trailing down her back?"

"Yes, I believe that's it," said Rebecca.

"I just dressed her this morning. She's beautiful isn't she, so modern but with a classic beauty."

"Yes, yes." Rebecca imagined Nora wearing the gown, being escorted down the aisle by her father. Kevin was waiting for her at the altar, decked out in a tuxedo.

"Excuse me, ma'am, would you like to order a fitting for someone?"

"Yes I would. I mean, I would like to but the time is not right... not just yet."

The clerk began leafing through a white book embossed with gold letters. "We offer a full set of services. We have invitations and discounts for the wedding party, limousine services, and free engagement planning. When will the wedding take place?"

"I think it will be soon. Do you have a card?"

The clerk handed her a card: *The Blushing Bridal Shop, one-stop shopping for all your bridal needs. Robert and Rosalie Blushing, proprietors.*

Rebecca tucked it into her pocket and turned to leave.

"We have a special," said the clerk. "It's twenty-percent off all flowers."

"We'll be in touch," said Rebecca. The feeling of anticipation was replaced with a warm glow of satisfaction. "Thank you, God," she said. "Thank you for lifting this burden from my heart."

She drove home and parked in the garage. When she entered the house, the telephone was ringing. It was her sister Maureen.

"How was the trip to Salt Lake?" asked Rebecca.

"It was great. We learned lots of new hymns and ate too much then Reverend Miller had to leave early because his wife was giving birth to a baby girl."

"That's wonderful. I'll have to contribute," said Rebecca. "Did anything else happen?"

"Let's see… do you remember Betty Jaworski?"

The name sounded familiar.

"I think Nora knows Kevin, her son?"

"Oh yes," said Rebecca.

"She said Kevin is coming home."

Rebecca was speechless for a few seconds, then whispered, "Praise the Lord."

"What?" said Maureen.

"You don't say. I thought he was on a mission in Ecuador."

"I know, I know. I didn't get much of a chance to talk with her, but I think he's coming back next week. I'll let you know when I find out more."

"That's wonderful. I'm sure Nora will want to know that."

"I have to go now," said Maureen. "Talk to you later."

After she hung up, Rebecca took the card from the wedding shop out of her pocket, held it next to her heart, and smiled.

She called Nora, but she wasn't home.

"Let's see," said Rebecca looking at her calendar. "Kevin is coming home next week and will probably need some time to unwind. Why is he coming home? Maybe he came down with some tropical disease. I hope it's nothing contagious," she frowned. "Oh, there I go again. I'll just need to trust in the Lord. If Kevin asks Nora to marry him sometime in the next month we can begin planning a wedding for June. We'd better put a deposit down on that dress." Rebecca picked up a notebook from her desk and began writing down the details that needed to be finalized, then she put down her pencil and took a sip of coffee. Her heart was racing.

"So much to do, and so little time."

———————◆———————

As Nora entered the counseling office on Monday morning, she stopped short of her desk. There in the middle was a cluster of roses in a vase. *The last time someone gave me roses was at my high school prom*, she thought.

She plucked a note from the plastic holder and opened the tiny envelope. "May our friendship continue, Thomas."

Whatever did that mean? Does he expect me to forget about what happened? I wish I could forget the whole thing like it was a bad movie. Thank God he's out of town for a week. Nora picked up the card. The printed greeting on the front read "Thinking of You" next to a face of a puppy dog. He had written the note inside in long-hand with a black pen. Some of the letters ran together and were poorly formed with large loops and irregular spacing.

She ripped up the note and threw it in the trash can. Then she picked up the vase and sneezed as she moved the flowers into Dr. Nederman's office.

Nora worked on the teaching schedule and fielded phone calls for most of the morning until she was caught up. She had some extra time, so decided to type a letter to her sister, June, who had recently married and was now pregnant.

She began typing, "Hi June, I just wanted to touch base with you to let you know I might be transferring to another department at the university." *Should I tell her why? I can't tell her the real reason. If I do, it will get back to Mother and pretty soon the whole family will know.* She deleted the sentence and started again. "I've been thinking of this for a long time and feel that it is time for a change. I'll be…"

Nora noticed the door open. A tall young man with long blond hair and a mustache walked in. She recognized him from her psychology class.

"How are you?" he grinned. "I didn't know you worked here."

"Yes," said Nora, smiling back. "I... I... I'm sorry, but I forgot your name."

"Zack, Zack Kincaid."

"Oh, that's right," said Nora. "How are you, Zack?"

"Pretty good, now let me see... I think I remember your name... It starts with 'N'... yes, yes... I'm sure it starts with 'N.'"

Nora began to blush. "My name... "

"No, no don't tell me. I've almost got it." Zack put his index finger in the air, looked at the ceiling and said, "Nora. I think that's it: Nora."

"Yes. Yes, that's it!" said Nora, beaming.

"I've never met anyone named Nora. That's a beautiful name."

"I was named after my aunt." She felt her cheeks flush. "I used to think it was too old fashioned."

"No, no, it's great. It's unusual, but it has a lot of character."

"Why, thank you, Zack," Nora smiled and her heart quickened. *Oh my, I think I'm blushing. I haven't felt this way since the first time I saw Kevin at church.*

"What I came here for," said Zack, looking away, "was to get some information about the counseling program. Is Dr. Nederman in?"

"He's out until Wednesday," said Nora. "Are you thinking of getting into the program?"

"Yeah." Zack stroked his mustache. "Just thinking… trying to weigh some options." He cocked his head and sniffed the air, then looked around the room.

"What's wrong?" said Nora.

"Oh, nothing, I just thought I smelled roses but I don't see any."

"The… the florist was just here," Nora stammered. "He brought them to the wrong office."

"Oh, too bad. Can I pick up an application?"

Nora reached into her drawer and handed Zack a form.

Zack slowly lifted the sheet from her outstretched hand. "Thank you very much," he said. "I'll see you in class."

"Stop by Wednesday," said Nora. "I'll tell Dr. Nederman you were here."

After Zack left, Nora reached into her purse and took out her mirror. She dabbed on some lipstick and pursed her lips then brushed back a low hanging curl. Her smile broadened. *What has gotten into me?*

Nora had lunch with Susan Decker who had been working at the university for fifteen years and had mentored Nora when she first started five years earlier. Susan, a Native American with dark hair and a stocky build, was the head of the Clerical Workers Union.

"How's your day going?" asked Susan. She remembered how she had taken Nora shopping when she started working there. Nora had a habit of showing up for work in low cut necklines and miniskirts and Susan helped her pick out some more appropriate outfits.

"Thomas... I mean Dr. Nederman is out of town for a couple days, so I'm just holding down the fort," said Nora.

She poured some cream into her coffee and took a sip.

"So how is Thomas?" asked Susan. "Up to his old tricks?"

Nora began to choke on her coffee and brought a napkin to her mouth.

"Old tricks?" she said, catching her breath.

"Honey, I haven't been here fifteen years for nothing." Susan tooking a bite from her hamburger.

"I don't know what you mean. We have an excellent working relationship."

"Well, maybe I misspoke," said Susan. "Just watch out if he starts sending you flowers."

Nora sneezed. *Oh my God. Is she psychic?*

"What about the flowers?" asked Nora.

"We handled a complaint about five years ago from one of his secretaries. It was all very hush, hush. Nobody wanted it to get any further. Dr. Nederman started sending her flowers then began giving her back rubs—all very therapeutic of course," said Susan with a sneer.

"So what happened?"

"Her husband found out and came unglued. Of course Nederman claimed the whole thing was a big misunderstanding, but he had to get a restraining order against the guy. Eventually she was able to transfer to another department."

Nora opened her mouth to speak then stopped.

"You were going to say something?" Susan said slowly, staring straight into Nora's eyes.

"I guess I need to tell someone," Nora began. She took a deep breath. "Please don't repeat this to anyone."

Sue hesitated. "Okay."

Nora looked around then leaned over the table. "I'm getting a transfer out of the counseling department because I can't work there anymore."

"Why not?"

"Dr. Nederman gave me a neck-rub one day and…well…it turned into more than just a neck-rub." Nora leaned back, folded her arms around herself then took another deep breath and slowly exhaled. "I was so relaxed, just like the last time."

"You mean he had given you massages before?"

"Just once," Nora lied.

"But this time was different."

"Yes, this time he began to rub my..." she desperately grasped for a word. "...my front. I know I should have left, but I didn't. We did a lot more, too." Tears formed in Nora's eyes. "I don't know why I let it get so out of hand, but I did."

Susan reached across the table and took Nora's hand.

"It will be all right," she said gently. "What he did was wrong."

"But what I did was wrong, too," said Nora. "We were both wrong."

"Nora, this won't be the last time he tries that. He has created a hostile work environment. We can nail him. He's a predator."

Nora abruptly wiped her eyes. "No. I don't want this to get out. I don't want anyone to know about this."

"But Nora, you will remain anonymous. I'm sure the university will support you. You'll be doing everyone a huge favor."

"Who would know?"

"Just the members of the grievance committee, the Affirmative Action Officer and the Chancellor," said Susan. "Everything would remain *very* confidential."

No way, thought Nora. She looked at her watch. "I'll think about it." She picked up her tray. "I'd better get back to work."

"I understand," said Susan. "I don't want to pressure you. I'll check back with you later."

———————◆———————

Rebecca finally connected with Nora on the phone shortly after she arrived home from work.

"Hello darling. I've been calling all evening. Where have you been?"

"I had to do some shopping, mother," Nora said crisply.

"Well, get ready for some good news. I was talking with Maureen today and she said that Kevin is returning from Ecuador next week."

"Next week?" said Nora. "I wonder why he didn't say anything about it in his last letter. Why is he coming home so early?"

"I don't know all the details, but Maureen heard it from Kevin's mother. Isn't that wonderful? I'll bet he missed you more than you thought and just wanted to surprise you."

Nora smiled as she thought of Kevin wrapping his strong arms around her.

"I hope he's home to stay," said Nora.

"Have faith."

"Yes, Mother."

"I sense that you are beginning to feel the Holy Spirit. The vision was clear. God wants you and Kevin to be together.

"I... I... just wasn't sure," said Nora. "I didn't want to get my hopes up. I wanted Kevin to accomplish whatever he was trying to do. I've missed him, but I'm not sure he feels the same way about me."

"Of course he missed you. I don't know why he's coming back now but I know that's how God wants it to be."

"How can you be so sure?" said Nora.

"You'll see," said Rebecca.

Nora saw her mother smiling, her eyes wide and filled with certainty just like she had so many times in the past when she spoke of her visions.

"I'm sorry mother but I have some ice cream to put into the freezer," said Nora. "Let me know if you hear anything more."

Nora glanced at the couch where she and Kevin had kissed. A warm glow came over her. But as she unloaded the groceries, she caught the flowery aroma of some bar soap. That reminded her of the roses. The glow vanished.

She shook her head. *How could I have been so stupid?*

Tuesday morning, Nora went to the Human Resources and filled out a request for a transfer. There was an opening for an administrative assistant in the Math Department.

Dr. Nederman pulled his Corvette into the parking lot Wednesday morning and walked into the Education Building. When he entered his office, Nora was standing next to a file cabinet. He gave her a quick hug. She turned her face away and stiffened up.

"What's wrong? Is my favorite secretary having a bad day?"

Nora closed the file drawer and sat down at her desk. "I've got something to tell you." She glanced up. "I've been thinking about this for a long time and… and…"

"And you're feeling uncomfortable about our little indiscretion," said Nederman. "I'm not a psychologist for nothing, you know. I'd like to work through this with you if we could."

"I've applied for a transfer."

"A transfer?" Nederman's mouth fell open. "There's no need for you to leave. I assure you that nothing like… you know… that nothing will ever happen again. I think we both made a mistake, but I have to take most of the responsibility. I feel terrible about this and I'd like to make it up to you."

Nederman put his hands on Nora's desk and leaned forward. He looked around. "Let's go into the other room and try to work this out."

"I'm sorry about this too," said Nora, grimacing. The sweet smell of his cologne made her want to throw up. "I think a transfer is best for both of us."

Nederman lowered his head. "Well, it seems like your mind is made up," he said softly.

"I'm sorry, I just think—"

"I know. You're right. I should have used better judgment. I just hoped we could move on from there. I promise that nothing like that will ever happen again. I've been under a lot of stress lately and I let things go too far. But if you have to leave, I hope we can part company as friends," he said with a shy smile.

"Yes," Nora lied. "I'll always think of you as a… friend."

Dr. Nederman walked into his private office, slumped down in the padded chair next to his computer and smiled sadly. *I must be more careful next time.* He stared at the blue glow of a lava lamp sitting on a small table in the corner. Clumps of wax were changing shape as they slowly rose then fell in the hot oil. The lamp was a gift from his wife on their tenth wedding anniversary, a tongue in cheek comment on the Sixties. *Such a long time ago, the era of free love, sex for sex's sake.* He leaned forward and picked up the lamp. It was warm. He turned it over in his hands, inspecting it, then gently placed it back on the table. *So out of place now, like a relic from another time.*

◆

Sue Decker called Nora at home on Thursday to check on her emotional state.

"I'm fine, I guess," Nora said.

"Have you thought about what we talked about on Tuesday?"

"You mean about filing a complaint?"

"Yes."

"Well, I don't know. I really would rather transfer to another department and be done with it," said Nora.

"Are you sure?"

"Yes. I actually feel a little sorry for Dr. Nederman," said Nora. "He's kind of pathetic. I mean, he's in a marriage that doesn't satisfy him and he's reaching out in desperation to get comfort from someone who he's supposed to have a professional relationship with. He needs counseling as much as his clients do. He knows how to charm the students but, deep down inside I know he's hurting."

"Don't you see?" said Susan raising her voice. "That's all part of his *shtick*. He gets away with it because he makes these women feel sorry for him. He's a master manipulator and he's just going to go on wrecking lives until he's stopped."

"I'm really sorry," said Nora getting ready to leave. "I need to think of my own sanity. I just want to move on."

◆

"I have never been treated like this. Ten years in Women's Studies and I get bumped by someone with higher seniority," said Ruth Pritchard, a stocky woman with short brown hair who was Nora's replacement.

Nora rolled her eyes. This was the third time that morning Ruth

had mentioned her resentment at not getting a supervisory position. Nora checked her watch. *Only four hours left of breaking her
in and then I'll be free.*

They had lunch at the cafeteria.

"So what's he really like?" asked Ruth.

"You mean Dr. Nederman?" said Nora, looking in her mirror.
Something had fallen into her eye. Maybe it was a bit of mascara.

"Yes. Of course. Who did you think I meant?"

Nora wet a napkin in her water glass and carefully wiped the corner of her eye. "Oh yes, Dr. Nederman. He's very nice. You'll like
him once you get to know him."

"So what's with all those pictures in his office?" said Ruth.

"I'm not sure what you mean," said Nora. "Which pictures?"

"That picture of Freud," Ruth said with a sneer.

Nora had never given the pictures much thought. Dr. Nederman
had all kinds of pictures in his office. Besides the pictures of Alfred
Adler, C. G. Jung, Carl Rogers, Albert Ellis, he had one taken at
the Esalen Institute of himself and a bearded Fritz Perls in a hot
tub together.

"Freud is the father of modern psychotherapy," said Nora.

"Ha," grunted Ruth "Penis envy."

"I beg your pardon?"

"Penis envy," Ruth said again. "Freud believed that all women were suffering from penis envy and that's why they could never be complete human beings. That concept has done more violence to women than all the wars ever fought."

"Oh well," said Nora. "That was in the olden days. We've come a long way since then."

"Oh sure, a long ways," said Ruth. "Like Fritz Perls the sex pervert?"

"What on earth are you talking about?'

"I know what went on at his Esalen Institute in California," said Ruth, shaking her head in disgust. "The orgies and the psychedelic drugs. They call it treatment, but all that talk about hot tubs and massage therapy is just an excuse for immorality."

Nora sat there with her mouth open, then her look of surprise slowly changed to a smile. She leaned forward and gently patted Ruth's arm. "I think you'll find that the counseling department is much... different from what you're used to. I'm sure there is room for improvement. And I know you're just the right person to... influence the culture of the department in a positive direction."

11

Ménage à Trois

NORA'S NEW OFFICE WAS ON THE THIRD FLOOR of the physical sciences building, overlooking downtown. She could see the large metallic roundhouses of the Union Pacific rail yard and tracks leading south across bridges and around Scout Mountain, its lower elevations covered with sagebrush.

A PhD student, named Marilyn, who had been filling in until they could get a replacement, trained Nora in her new job. There were five professors in the small math department, but most of them were gone for the summer. Professor Yang remained to teach two summer courses in advanced trigonometry for engineering students.

Nora's first day on the job was slow. Most of the work involved processing student applications for the fall. It was difficult to concentrate because she was thinking about Kevin's return. *What should I wear to greet him?* she wondered. *Maybe something sexy that would show a little cleavage. It's certainly hot enough that a low–cut neckline won't seem too out of the ordinary. He's been gone for two months. Maybe he'll be ready for a little romance and we can start over again.*

Suddenly Nora had a disturbing thought. What if he'd had relations with other women? A scowl crossed her face. Maybe he'd found someone else. But two months wasn't much time to get to know someone, she reasoned. Besides, he was probably too busy with the irrigation project. In the end, she decided she would just have to trust in God. Kevin's plane might even be in the air right now. Nora closed her eyes. She could almost see him smile and hold out his arms as he rushed toward her.

She heard a voice. "Nora."

"Yes."

Professor Yang had somehow materialized before her.

"I'm sorry to interrupt. It looked like you were really concentrating on those applications."

"Yes. Yes, I was."

"That's good. You're doing a wonderful job. I just wanted you to know I'll be out of the office. I have a meeting with a visiting professor and won't be back until tomorrow."

"I hope your meeting goes well. See you tomorrow," Nora smiled.

After work Nora stopped by the grocery store. As she passed the wine display she noticed a woman giving out samples of Ménage à Trois wine. She tasted a small plastic cup full. It went down easy, so she bought two bottles, one to share with Kevin.

When Nora got home, she changed into some shorts, poured

herself a glass of wine then lay down on the couch to watch her favorite soap opera, *All My Children*.

In the current episode, Erica was trying to seduce Steve, the son of her ex-lover, to get back at him for dumping her. The young man had just gotten out of jail after four years, having been framed by his twin brother who had been having an affair with Erica's niece.

Nora had a sip of wine, then another.

Erica, dressed in a low-cut evening gown, was on a couch in her penthouse with Steve, whom she had lured up with the offer of a job. "The Girl from Ipanema" was playing on the stereo as Erica slipped closer to her prey. She gave Steve a sultry kiss and began massaging his shoulders.

"I'm so glad to see you," she cooed. "It must have been the worst thing in the world to be in prison for four long years. I'd like to help you re-enter society, if you'll let me."

"What about the job?" asked Steve.

"Oh yes… the job. How silly of me to forget. How would you like to be my very personal limousine driver?"

Steve grinned.

In the next scene they were in bed together. Steve kissed Erica's neck, then his head disappeared from view. Erica sighed.

"Mmmmmm…" purred Nora as she lightly ran her fingers down the inside of her leg. Suddenly she stopped. *I shouldn't be doing this,* she thought.

Steve's head and naked chest reappeared.

"You're a wonderful lover," sighed Erica. "I just hope you are discreet."

"Don't worry," said Steve. "I never kiss and tell."

Nora moved her other hand to her breast and began lightly stroking her nipple. She was overcome with a need to satisfy herself and she looked around. *Why should I stop when there's no one here?*

Erica flirted with Steve, lightly kissing the corners of his mouth, then moving to his neck. She put her arms around his smooth muscular back and ran her finger down his spine.

Nora began to feel wet.

The screen cut to a commercial but Nora felt too good to stop. She unbuttoned her blouse and loosened her bra strap. She imagined herself alone with Kevin in a cabana somewhere in South America. They had drinks then walked down the beach to a deserted spot where the coconut smell of their suntan lotion mixed with salty air. Gulls played in the wind and made soft cawing noises. Kevin kissed her.

"I'm glad we're finally alone together," he said massaging her breasts

Nora closed her eyes and began rubbing herself. It didn't take long.

"Oh God," she cried as waves of passion rolled over her body. She slowly removed her hand and let the pleasure subside.

Afterward, she relaxed and refocused on the TV screen but they had cut to a commercial. She refastened her bra, then glanced up at the open blind.

"Damn, damn, damn." She stood up and looked outside. A woman was walking toward the apartment building with a little girl. Nora closed the blinds and felt a flush of embarrassment. *If I had climaxed two minutes later they might have heard me.* She finished her glass of wine and corked the bottle.

After a shower, she watched the news and weather. The heat wave was supposed to break as soon as thundershowers moved into the area.

Earl was laid up with a bout of pneumonia and Rebecca was fixing dinner for him but every time the phone rang she rushed to pick it up. She had her spies out and was hoping for news of Kevin's arrival.

Michelle Phillips, who ran a temporary help agency, knew who was having parties. Certainly, Kevin's mother will throw a party for him when he gets back, thought Rebecca. *We'll grab an invite, and after the crowd thins out, Kevin and Nora can be alone together. Maybe he will ask her to marry him.*

Another spy was one of Kevin's neighbors who used to baby sit Nora. Millie Dugan was getting on in years, but had always been reliable for gossip. She had a window facing Kevin's parent's house and had been instructed to call Rebecca as soon as Kevin arrived

Rebecca spooned some mashed potatoes and applesauce onto Earl's plate along with some puréed beef. He hadn't eaten much for several days. She brought the food into the living room where he was watching a basketball game on TV and set it on a tray next to Earl's armchair.

"Here's some food, dear. I know you're not hungry but you have to try to eat."

"You're right about me not being hungry," Earl said. Suddenly, he began coughing and grabbed a tissue.

"You poor dear," comforted Rebecca.

Earl slowly pushed himself up from the chair and trudged into the bathroom where he coughed until he his face turned purple. When he took his hand away from his mouth there was blood in the tissue. He threw the tissue into the toilet and flushed, took a deep breath, and returned to the living room.

"Are you all right, dear?"

"I'll be just fine, just need a little sip of brandy to calm things down."

"That's the last thing you need, Earl Fairchild, and you know it." Rebecca ran into the bathroom and grabbed a bottle of cough medicine.

"Just take some of this and you'll feel better." She carefully placed the bottle on his tray.

"I've tried and it just doesn't work," he said, then began another coughing spasm.

When he regained his composure, he looked at the medicine bottle. "All right, all right, I guess that's better than nothin'."

◆

Earl had been sober for most of their marriage and Rebecca had thanked God for that. She had kept a close watch on him, taking him to work every morning and picking him up at night. But after he retired and the girls moved out, Earl would often go down to the rail yards and share a bottle with friends after work. One day, Earl came home from the yards with alcohol on his breath. He sat down on his Lazy-boy recliner and switched on the TV. Rebecca had confronted him.

"Earl, I want you to turn off that set and pray with me," she said.
"About what?"
"Earl, I think you know."
Earl raised the remote and flicked off the TV.
"I guess you busted me. I had a couple beers with the boys down at the yard. Been meaning to talk with you about it but it never

seemed to be the right time."

"Earl, please pray with me." Rebecca knelt down in front of him. She took his hands. "Jesus, this is a good man who only wants to do your bidding and walk in your light. Bow your head, Earl. Jesus, this man has been tempted by Satan, and while he wants to walk the way of righteousness, he is weak. Oh Jesus, he is weak but he is good. So I ask you in your Father's name to help heal this man and make him whole. Our Father who art in heaven, hallowed be Thy name… pray with me, Earl."

Earl began to murmur.

"Louder, Earl. The Lord has to be able to hear you. Thy kingdom come, thy will be done, on earth as it is in heaven."

They began to pray louder, their voices blending into one. "Give us this day our daily bread and forgive us our trespasses as we forgive those who trespass against us."

"Yes, Earl, yes. Jesus is listening!" Rebecca's voice was joyous. "And lead us not into temptation but deliver us from evil, for Thine is the kingdom and the power and glory forever and ever. Amen. Say Amen, Earl."

"Amen," said Earl.

As she held Earl's hand, she felt a peace descend on her. Outside, a breeze rustled in the trees as the sun came out from behind a dark cloud.

"The Lord has heard our prayer," she said.

But Earl kept on drinking. He hid pints of whisky around the house and when Rebecca emptied them into the toilet he'd just go out and buy some more. She introduced him to a former alcoholic from church, names Tom. Earl agreed to attend an Alcoholics Anonymous meeting with him. At the meeting he saw people getting up and admitting they were alcoholics. The next week Earl admitted that he, too, was an alcoholic. Tom helped him reconnect with his higher power, work the Twelve Steps, and swear off alcohol.

Rebecca thanked God, Jesus and The Holy Ghost for their divine intervention. Earl was sober again, but Rebecca knew that Satan would return to tempt him.

◆

Millie Dugan called Friday night and said she had seen Kevin getting out of the car with his parents and another woman she couldn't identify.

Rebecca was thrilled. He was finally home. The other woman was probably one of Kevin's sisters. Millie's eyesight was not the best and Kevin's sister had been away at college for a long time.

She called Nora immediately and told her the good news.

"Why don't you go over there and welcome him home."

"I don't know," said Nora. "Maybe we... I should let him

get settled."

"Don't be silly. I'm sure he wants to see you."

"Mother," Nora said, "it's ten o'clock and I'm sure Kevin has had a long trip. I can give him a call in the morning."

"Oh, of course, dear. You're probably right."

That night Nora had trouble falling asleep. *Why didn't Kevin let me know he was home? Did he get sick? Did the church call him back?*

Saturday morning Nora called, but Kevin's line was busy. Her mother stopped over and they decided to go shopping and pick up a welcome home card for Kevin.

They pulled into the mall and parked near the Target department store.

"Let's go in here," said her mother. "Before we get a card, I want to look at some plastic wear for the reception... I mean the church picnic this summer."

Nora followed her mother through the doors and down an aisle toward a large display of elegant plates and utensils.

"How do you like these?" said her mother, holding up a package of 50 transparent plates engraved with swirls of flowers.

"I don't think we need something that elegant for the picnic, Mother."

Nora looked around, noticed another table with paper plates and began walking toward it, then stopped. A lean suntanned man wearing a tee shirt and shorts was walking toward her.

"Kevin?" she called. "Kevin, is that you?"

Kevin walked over and gave her a friendly hug. "A little tired but doing fine. How are you doing? We just flew in last night."

Nora's mother looked up and gave Kevin a broad smile.

"I guess I should have called but everything has been so crazy since we arrived," said Kevin.

"We heard you were coming in this weekend but we didn't know when," said Rebecca, smiling from ear to ear.

Just then a young woman with dark eyes and a copper bracelet came down the escalator and walked over to Kevin.

"Oh, here you are," she said with a Spanish accent, smiling at Nora and her mother. "Are these friends of yours?"

"Yes…yes they are," said Kevin. "This is Nora and her mother, Mrs. Fairchild."

The woman smiled. "I'm very happy to meet you."

Nora and her mother smiled back. "And your name is?" asked Rebecca.

"Oh… sorry… this is Maria," apologized Kevin.

"We are getting married," said Maria, beaming at Kevin.

Nora and her mother froze.

"Did I forget to tell you about Maria in my letters?" said Kevin.

"Yes, you did," said Nora, her smile fading.

"My God," said Rebecca. "How could you have possibly forgotten to let us know?"

Nora turned to her mother and mouthed the words *not now.*

"I'm so sorry, but everything happened so fast," stammered Kevin. "Maria's visa came through and she was accepted to grad school here."

"Yes," said Maria. "I'm going to start school in the fall. Isn't that wonderful?"

Nora shot a glance at her mother, but said nothing.

"Well, we have to go now," said Kevin. "We'll all have dinner sometime and you can see our pictures when I get them developed. Talk to you later."

"It was very nice meeting you both," smiled Maria.

Nora and her mother watched silently as Kevin and Maria walked through the sliding glass doors leading to the parking lot. Rebecca's fingers were still locked onto the package of transparent plates engraved with little swirls of flowers.

12

Scout Mountain

ZACK HAD BEEN WATCHING NORA FOR A LONG TIME. She usually made it to class just before the lecture started, smelling of perfume and dressed impeccably, and took a seat in the back of the classroom. Zack always made a point to try and sit next to her. After class, they would make casual conversation as they walked to the parking lot.

"I have a list of topics I would like the class to work on in small groups," Professor Blackburn announced before handing out assignments. "You can pick any topic you want."

Zack turned to Nora. "Do you want to team up?"

Nora smiled. "Sure, that would be great."

After class they read the list together.

"Do any of these topics interest you?" asked Zack.

Nora looked at the list. "Why don't you pick something?"

"All right," said Zack. He scanned the list. *This one might be just up her alley.*

"Is 'Social Anxiety and Non-Assertiveness' okay with you?"

"I guess so," she said slowly.

They made plans to get together at the campus library

Sunday afternoon.

Zack arrived at the library early and located a study in *The Social Psychology Journal* on social assertiveness training.

Yes, this will do... just right. Make a few notes... move on to other things... beautiful day for a drive.

Nora arrived wearing a tank top, black shorts, and slippers with straps across the tops. Her legs were pale and her face was without the heavy make-up Zack was used to seeing in class. She nodded and smiled as she entered, then sat down sat down next to him.

"I've been going through a couple of these journals and this may be what we're looking for," said Zack. He could smell a hint of her perfume. The loose curls in her hair spread out on her bare shoulders. He turned the opened journal toward her and moved a little closer.

"Here's something we can use." He pointed to a passage and began reading; "Controlled experiments with socially anxious patients indicate that the most efficacious treatment modalities involve systematic desensitization combined with behavior rehearsal..." He stopped and let her read the rest, then leaned back and draped his arm across the back of her chair.

Nora's eyes scanned the next few pages, which described several treatments for the disorder. Zack read over her shoulder. He could see that there was a lot to cover.

"Why don't we split it up and we can each do a treatment modality then combine our work," he said.

Nora smiled. "That sounds like a good idea. I'll copy the pages and then we'll take them home and write it up."

As they left the library, Zack pointed out the top of Scout Mountain on the horizon and suggested they visit it. Nora agreed and soon they were driving up through switchbacks on the side of the mountain. They stopped at a campground and took a walk along a path with yellow spring flowers and a little stream running along the side.

About a half-mile into their hike, the trail crossed another small stream. Zack picked his way across the rocks first then offered his hand to Nora, who carefully stepped from rock to rock. When she reached the other side, she took Zack's hand and almost slipped. He pulled her toward him and gave her a little hug. He drank in the warmth as he felt her body against his, if only for a moment.

"Are you okay?"

"I'm just fine," she smiled.

They walked down the trail arm in arm. The air smelled of sweet tamarack and the sun sparkled off little eddies in the stream as it gurgled and sang its way toward the valley.

When Zack dropped her off in the parking lot at the university, they exchanged telephone numbers.

———————◆———————

Rebecca slowly scraped the uneaten portions of Earl's dinner down the garbage disposal and washed the plate off, thinking all the time about what had happened at the mall. No matter how she tried to frame it, one thing was clear—Kevin was going to marry someone else. *Or was he? Maybe something would happen to change that. Maybe... oh no...* She didn't want to think about something happening to Maria. *She seemed like such a sweet girl... yet... God had given her a vision.*

Just then she heard Earl begin coughing, followed by a crash. She dropped the plate in the sink and ran into the living room. Earl was lying on the floor clutching his chest.

"Dear God," said Rebecca. She ran over to him and knelt down. "Earl, can you hear me?"

She managed to roll him on his side. Earl looked up at her. "I think I'm having a heart attack." His face contorted with pain and his eyes were starting to bulge out.

Rebecca dialed 911.

She pulled the phone to where Earl was lying. "Help is on the way, Honey. Don't worry. Everything's going to be all right." Earl was starting to turn blue and his breathing was irregular. Rebecca cradled his head in her lap and asked the 911 operator to pray with her. "Dear God, I pray to you, spare the life of this man. His work on this earth is not done. Please, in the name of Jesus I pray."

Earl's eyes rolled back in his sockets and he began shaking.

"Oh, Dear God," cried Rebecca. "Please don't let him die."

Earl was unconscious but still breathing when the paramedics arrived. They quickly took his vital signs and loaded him onto a stretcher.

"Have faith in the Lord, dear," Rebecca called as the ambulance pulled out, siren blasting.

Rebecca called Nora and left a message on her answering machine, then rode to ER with a policeman. When they arrived, she approached a nurse in blue surgical scrubs who was sitting behind a glassed-in area.

"Excuse me," she said.

The nurse looked up.

"My husband was just brought in here by ambulance. Earl Fairchild?"

The nurse looked at a clipboard in front of her.

"Just a minute," she said, dialing a number.

She turned away from Rebecca, who could hear snatches of conversation, "Yes, she's here... don't think so... just arrived a few minutes ago... yes... okay."

She turned back to Rebecca. "Please, have a seat. Someone will be out shortly."

"How is he? Can I see him?"

"The doctor will be out in a minute. Please just have a seat," said the nurse, gesturing to the waiting room.

Rebecca went into a small room with a TV and a couple couches and sat down. Just then Nora walked in and they embraced. While she was telling Nora what happened, a young doctor wearing a surgical gown walked into the room.

"Are you the family of Earl Fairchild?" he asked.

"How is he?" asked Rebecca. "Can we see him?"

"We did all we could, but it wasn't enough," said the doctor. "I'm very sorry, but your husband had a massive heart attack. He never regained consciousness."

Nora put her arm around her mother as she began sobbing.

"You can see him now, if you would like," said the doctor.

Over two hundred people came to the funeral service. The burial was at the Holy Resurrection Cemetery on the west side of town on a nicely terraced spot half way up the side of a mountain. As Earl was being lowered into the ground, a gust of wind blew a cloud of dust toward the mourners.

Nora's mother smiled sadly as she touched the casket. She wiped a tear from her eye, looked at the other side of the valley, and smiled, knowing that Earl's spirit was now in the arms of a loving God.

———————◆———————

After Nora dropped her sister and brother-in-law at the airport, she drove her mother home. Nora had temporarily moved back in keep her company.

While Rebecca changed clothes, Nora sat on the couch and wondered what her mother would do without Earl.

She went downstairs and looked at her father's special room, the one where he smoked his cigarettes and kept all the memorabilia of his thirty-five years with the Union Pacific Railroad. She picked up a photo of four men standing in front of an old steam engine. Her father was the one on the end with overalls and suspenders. He had his arm around the shoulders of the man next to him and was smoking a cigarette.

"Those damn cancer sticks," Nora whispered. "He just couldn't quit."

Suddenly the sadness hit her. Her father was never coming home. She buried her face in her hands and cried.

After dabbing her eyes, she went upstairs. Her mother was sitting on the couch and staring out the picture window that faced the cemetery on the other side of the valley.

Nora sat down next to her. "How are you doing, Mother?"

"I was just thinking."

"About what?"

"Your father visited me in my dreams last night. He said he was going to be in heaven with the Lord and that I shouldn't worry about his soul." She turned to her daughter and smiled sadly. "Did you know I occasionally worried about your father's soul?"

"I think everyone worries about their soul sometimes."

"Yes, yes, of course," said her mother turning back to the window. She bit her lip as if she was about to cry, then smiled. "But your father was a good man and I prayed for him every day—every day of his life."

Nora remembered how her father used to sit next to her mother in church and reach over occasionally to hold her hand. *She must miss him terribly.*

She moved closer and put her arm around her mother. Suddenly, her mother began to cry and Nora pulled her closer.

"I know we just have to trust that God has a plan for us and he loves us," her mother said as Nora handed her a tissue. "We must have faith." She looked up at Nora. "You need to have faith, too, that God still wants you and Kevin to be together."

"Let's not talk about that now, Mother."

"God sometimes does things we don't understand. Maybe Kevin has to go through a phase before he can really appreciate what you have to offer. Maybe he's not quite ready. I have a feeling that God is preparing him for you."

"I don't know, Mother, maybe you are right." Nora felt very tired and got up. "Would you like some coffee?"

"That would be nice."

Nora put a filter in the coffeemaker, filled it with two scoops of coffee and poured water into the reservoir. She pushed the button and went back into the living room. Nora sat down on the couch and looked at her mother's face. She was beginning to worry about her. Her mother had dark circles under her eyes and her face was lined with deep wrinkles. The coffee machine began making little gurgling noises.

"Do you remember the Fields?" asked Rebecca.

"The couple who run the day care program at church?"

"Yes, that's them. Did you know its Fred's second marriage?"

"No."

"Oh yes. Fred once told me he had fallen in love with a woman who was a bit of a hippy. She was from back East and they met at a rock concert somewhere. Anyway, they used to go hitchhiking together all over the country, camping out and staying with friends, getting involved with drugs. Pretty soon this woman, oh what was her name... Something strange like a bird... Oh yes... I remember now... Raven... anyway where was I...?"

"They were traveling all over."

"Yes, well they decided to settle down together and raise a family. They had two children, the cutest little girls you could imagine. They joined a church and things went well for a while, but soon they started having arguments about how to raise the children. Fred wanted them baptized, but Raven objected. Raven began reverting to her old self, taking off for days at a time without telling Fred where she had been. She started doing drugs and one day she ran off with another man. Fred was left with two little children to raise."

"I remember Fred," said Nora. "He seemed like a nice guy."

"He is. I even thought that you and he would someday… oh well, never mind… anyway, every day he asked God to send him a wife and every day he was disappointed, but he kept on praying. Do you know how long he had to wait?"

"I didn't know he was praying for a woman," said Nora.

"Ten years. Can you imagine that? Ten years but he didn't give up because he had faith."

The aroma of fresh coffee filled the room. Nora poured two cups, then brought them into the living room. She felt a flash of anger.

She briskly set the cup and saucer on the table in front of her mother.

"I can't wait for ten years, Mother."

"Oh dear… no…no… I didn't mean that. I only wanted to give

you hope. I'm sure you won't have to wait that long. Oh dear no."

Nora put two teaspoons of sugar in her coffee.

"I suppose that Kevin and Maria could end up getting divorced," Rebecca continued. "Certainly, divorce is common these days and Kevin and Maria do come from different cultures. God has a plan for us all." Nora's mother smiled and nodded her head up and down. "Our faith will be rewarded. Just go about your life and He will take care of everything."

13

The Cruel God

ZACK DROVE THROUGH THE NARROW WINDING STREETS of the small close-knit neighborhoods of Blackfoot on the way home from work. He felt a longing as he looked at the pick-up trucks and smoke rising from the chimneys of the snug family houses. He recalled the joy of running home from elementary school once and showing his mother an "A" he had received on a spelling test. She had been baking cookies and when they came out of the oven she frosted one and gave it to him. It was warm and sweet. His mother hugged him and commented on what a smart boy she had. His sister was in her high chair making a mess of her apple sauce. He and his mother laughed about that, then posted the spelling test on the bulletin board for his father to see when he returned from work.

When he was thirteen, Zack was confirmed in the Catholic Church. He remembered how he knelt at the altar as the Bishop touched Zack's forehead with the holy water. Then, as the Bishop placed his hand on Zack's shoulder, Zack felt a soothing rush of energy. The Bishop pronounced the sacred Latin words which sealed Zack with the gift of the Holy Spirit. It was a sacrament of Zack's commitment to seeking a deeper understanding of God's grace. He became marked as God's property, a person set apart.

Zack was fourteen when his mother died. She had gone to the hospital to deliver her third child and never returned. After the funeral, family members helped with finances but gradually Zack's world began to fall apart. His father still took him and his sister to church and, as the priest read the morning sermon, Zack would fold his hands, lower his head, and ask God why He had to take his mother. The longer he prayed the more he despaired.

Zack threw himself into his studies and was offered a scholarship to the University of Wisconsin in Madison. He majored in psychology, because he felt the need to connect with other people.

Now, he wished he had never been confirmed. He wanted to wash the confirmation out of his body, that thing that set him apart from others, the lie that was implanted when he was too young to understand. Life just happened and no amount of praying could change it. If there was a God, He was a cruel god. Now Zack preferred to think that there was no God at all.

When he got home, Zack turned up the heat and fed Otis. His answering machine was blinking. It was his father.

"Hi, Zack," it began. "I haven't heard from you in a while and just thought we could touch base. Give me a call."

Zack slumped into a stuffed chair and lit a cigarette. It was the first time he had heard from his father in several months. He picked up the phone then put it down, not sure what to say. His father had a very successful law practice and had remarried soon after Zack's mother died. He encouraged Zack to accept his new wife but Zack refused to call her "mother." He immersed himself in his studies, waiting for the day he could leave home for college.

Nora pulled her car out of the driveway and headed down the hill toward the Mathematics Department. She had taken a week off, but was glad to leave her mother's house and looked forward to the distraction of work.

When she arrived, Professor Yang offered his condolences and brought her up to date on what had been going on. There was a pile of mail stacked neatly on her desk and she decided she would tackle that first.

Nora was opening letters when the door opened and an attractive dark-haired young woman walked in.

Nora looked up. "Can I help... " she froze in mid-sentence.

The young woman smiled. "Oh... Hello Nora. I didn't know you worked here. I'm Maria. We met at the mall."

Nora tried to smile. "Oh yes. Maria."

"Kevin told me about your father. I was so sorry to hear about his passing."

"Yes, well thank you. And how is Kevin?"

"He's still looking for a job, but I'm sure he'll find one soon. He's waiting in the car. I just wanted to pick up my schedule."

"Your schedule?" gasped Nora.

"Yes… oh I guess you didn't know." Maria smiled. "I'll be a graduate student here in the fall."

"Yes, that's… wonderful." Nora felt her chest tighten.

"I'm staying with Kevin's mother until we get married and can find our own place to live."

Nora looked at the pile of unfinished work on her desk then turned back to Maria. "I'm sorry, but I haven't had time to get the schedules printed. I should have them done in a couple days, so check back then."

"Okay," said Maria. "We'll have you over some night when we get settled. I guess we'll be seeing a lot of each other. Nice seeing you again."

After Maria left, Nora took a deep breath and slowly exhaled. *Is God punishing me for having the affair? What would have happened if I never had the affair? Maybe Kevin and Maria never would have met. Does God actually dabble in such trivialities or do these things just happen?*

———————◆———————

Billy Butts was awakened by the therapy tech shouting, "Drop your cocks and grab your socks." Billy rubbed the sleep from his eyes and sat up on the edge of his cot. "Retired Navy asshole," he muttered as he pulled on his pants.

He poked his head out of his room and gave James the finger. When Billy had been sentenced to another stint on Silverman IV, he had planned on becoming a model patient, let his disability payments accumulate then apply for discharge in six months. But things were becoming intolerable. His girlfriend Linda hadn't visited him in weeks and had even stopped sending him care packages. His psychiatrist was out of town and now, this wake up thing.

Billy went to the bathroom, stopping at the nurses' station on the way to get a cigarette. No one was there. *Shit! The service on this unit sucks.*

Finally James showed up, unlocked the cabinet and slowly extracted one cigarette from a pack.

"Here," he said, handing it to Billy. "Last one you get this morning."

After James lit it, Billy blew the smoke in his face and waited for a response but James ignored him.

"Hey, have a nice day," said Billy sarcastically. He turned and walked into the dayroom.

The unit was on shutdown, a tool the staff used to reassert control. Patients were not rewarded for positive behavior with increased privileges. There was no TV, so several patients were sitting in the lounge staring at the wall waiting for the breakfast trays.

Billy took a leak then slumped down on the couch in the day-room. Suddenly, he heard the clang of a metal gate closing and the hum of the elevator as it slowly made its way up to the unit.

"Stand back," shouted James, as the elevator doors opened and a worker pushed out a tall slotted cart holding the breakfast trays.

Billy snuffed out his cigarette and placed it behind his ear. Had the unit not been on shutdown, he would have used it to barter. After breakfast he noticed a sign on the bulletin board: PASTORAL COUNSELING 10 A.M. IN THE ACTIVITY ROOM.

Normally he wouldn't have anything to do with ministers. He thought they were just another part of the system that had screwed him over. But now he had a different idea and smiled to himself at its brilliance. *What if I can convince the priest that I want to reconnect with my faith? Maybe I can get an early discharge from this place of retards and idiots.*

At precisely 9:55 a.m. the hospital chaplain, Father Charles Meyer, entered Silverman IV. Even though the unit was on shutdown, he had successfully argued that barring his visit would violate the hospital's own policy of encouraging patients to practice their faith.

Before becoming chaplain at State Hospital South, Father Meyer enjoyed being pastor of a small parish on the Shoshone-Bannock Reservation. However, after two years he developed a severe skin rash due to the intense sun and fine dust that blew in from the desert. Although he hated the thought of leaving, he requested a transfer.

Father Meyer had studied each patient's chart and had written down their religious preference. Many had none. Most had troubled childhoods and impulse control issues, but he felt that if he could redeem even one soul, the Lord would be pleased. Of course, he didn't refer to the improvement as redemption. No, no, no. That wouldn't fly well with the secular state administration. He talked about the process of reintegrating the patient into the community, of giving them support and hope.

Father Meyer walked up to Irene, who was filing her nails in the glassed in area behind the nurse's station.

"Good morning," he said with a cheery smile.

Irene looked up. "Hello, Father," she said. "Have a seat."

Father Meyer sat down. "How are you doing with the shutdown?" he asked. He held a secret scorn for behavior modification programs because he believed they only treated the symptoms, not the cause, which was a spiritual vacuum.

Irene looked through the glass. "They are certainly quiet," she said with a smug smile. "They are supposed to come up with their own set of rules, their own government for the unit. So far we haven't seen a lot of progress."

"Let's hope they'll come up with something." Father Meyer sighed.

He had seen too many plans. As soon as the patients came up with a new form of governance for themselves, it began to fail. Rules were modified, inconsistently enforced and manipulated until the staff had no alternative but to shut the program down again. "Do you have anyone who wants to see me today?" he asked.

"Let me see," said Irene. She placed her nail file on the table and walked over to the clipboard on the door. It was blank.

"No, I don't believe we do," she said, holding up the list. "We put up a sign over there," she said somewhat defensively, pointing to the wall. "It's been up there for a week."

Father Meyer looked at the wall and saw a young man with wiry brown hair waving at him. Father Meyer waved back and turned to Irene.

"Is that... that... oh I can't remember his name," he said.

"Billy," said Irene, turning a bottle of nail polish remover upside down on a cotton ball.

"It appears that he's signaling to me." Father Meyer stood up and walked into the hallway.

"How are you today, Billy?"

"I could be better, but I guess I'll just have to stay here for a while." Billy forced a laugh.

Father Meyer raised his eyebrows. "I didn't see your name on the list this morning."

Billy hung his head. "Well, sir, to be perfectly honest with you, I hadn't decided to sign up until now."

"It's never too late," said Father Meyer, smiling. He knew that Billy's mother was Catholic, but his father was not. Over the years, his parents had argued a lot about which faith to raise their son in, until they divorced when Billy was twelve. Billy started having problems with truancy from school and was treated for everything from depression to generalized behavior disorders. After he had legally become an adult, he ended up in the State Prison in Boise for assaulting a therapist. Billy's mother pleaded with her son to contact Father Meyer, but until now her son had refused.

"Why don't we go into the office and have a talk," said Father Meyer.

They walked down the wide corridor and entered a small room with a couch and two stuffed chairs. The room was lit with an overhead florescent light and furnished with a small bookcase which held some magazines and a few tattered books.

Father Meyer sat on the couch and motioned toward the chair. "Please, have a seat."

Billy locked his hands behind his head then leaned back and crossed his legs. He sensed that the priest was a little man who needed to bring someone to God as much as Billy wanted to get out of Silverman IV. Billy took a deep breath and relaxed. *This is going to be like taking candy from a baby.*

14

Lava Hot Springs

THE CAR WINDOWS WERE WIDE OPEN AND ZACK'S LONG HAIR was whipping in the wind. The sun was setting and he could see the dark silhouettes of ancient volcanoes about fifty miles to the west. When he reached the Bannock-Shoshone trading post at Ft. Hall, he pulled off the road to get an Indian taco—a spicy concoction of hamburger and hot Jalapeño sauce heaped on a large piece of fry bread. After he was done eating, Zack doused the fire in his gut with a can of Pepsi and pulled back onto the highway. He had the weekend off.

On Saturday, he picked up Nora and they drove to Lava Springs, a small town east of Pocatello with a public swimming pool built over a hot spring.

It was a sunny day and Nora wore white shorts over a low cut bathing suit.

"This is a great day for a drive," said Zack as the road began to loop around the high hills on the way out of town.

"It's good to be out," said Nora. "I just had to get away."

"I know how you feel," said Zack. "It was the same when my mother died. After a while you have to start living again."

Nora scooted closer to Zack and he put his arm around her.

"I've decided to take some more counseling courses next semester," said Zack.

"That's great," said Nora. "What will you be taking?"

"I signed up for Fundamentals of Counseling. I talked with Dr. Nederman a couple weeks ago and he said it was a good course to start out with. I saw someone else at your desk. Are you still working there?"

"Oh no," said Nora. "I transferred."

"Why did you transfer?" asked Zack. He was disappointed because he had been looking forward to seeing Nora from time to time after their course ended.

Nora quickly pointed to a ridge that ran parallel to the road. "See that little rise? That used to be the Oregon Trail. The ruts from the wagon wheels are still there."

Zack shook his head, "Amazing." He wondered why she wouldn't tell him why she transferred.

As they drove up a hill, the trail cut crossed the road then disappeared into a gully.

"You really know a lot about the area," said Zack.

"Well, I should. I've lived here all my life. Every schoolchild knows about the Oregon Trail."

"It's new to me," said Zack.

"You said you came from Texas?"

"Yeah, I lived in Austin for a while. Then ended up in Wisconsin."

"I have family in West Virginia, but we never visit them," said Nora.

"You have it all right here, the mountains, the desert, the desert the mountains." He looked at Nora and they both laughed.

"You're teasing me," she said.

"No, really, it's beautiful. I've always wanted to live out west."

"I've always wanted to go east," said Nora.

"Don't bother. You have it all here."

Zack's warm hand on her bare shoulder made her smile. The sadness of her father's death had taken its toll, but now she began to feel life flowing back into her.

When they arrived at the town, Nora asked him to stop at a small park. They walked to a small patch of weeds.

"I want to show you something," said Nora.

"Oh, what a fine weed patch this is," joked Zack.

"No, it's over here."

Zack trudged half-way up a little rise to a bubbling spring.

"You can make soft drinks with this," said Nora.

Zack bent down, scooped up a little water in his hand and took a sip. "It tastes a little like tonic water."

"My father used to bring me here when I was a little girl. We'd bring limes and make ourselves a cocktail," said Nora, staring into the spring. Bits of vegetation rose with the thermal flow then slowly drifted back down.

"Sorry, I forgot the gin," said Zack.

"Actually, I prefer vodka," said Nora. "Come on, let's go for a swim."

She grabbed Zack's hand and they headed back to the car.

They drove only a short distance before they rounded a curve and Zack spotted a swimming complex located at the base of a treeless hill topped by clusters of broken rocks. Clouds of sulfurous smelling steam rose from the water.

After showering, Zack met Nora at the pool. He dove in but Nora walked down the cement steps in the shallow end. She was wearing a blue one piece bathing suit and without her make-up she reminded Zack of a little girl with large breasts.

When she made her way through waist high water to where Zack was standing, he playfully splashed some water her way.

She put up her hands. "Stop, I don't want to get my hair wet."

"Sorry," said Zack. He dove underwater and swam toward her. He saw her feet back peddling and scooped her into his arms then carried her out into deeper water.

"I hope you can swim," said Zack.

"I certainly can," said Nora. She tickled his ribs until he dropped her. They swam to the side of the pool where Zack gave her a hug. She gave him a quick kiss and pushed away, then swam to the ladder and climbed out. They found a picnic table on the grass. After lunch, they put their towels down and sunned themselves until it was time to leave.

While driving home, Nora snuggled up beside Zack. It was getting dark when they pulled into Nora's parking lot. It was still early and Nora wasn't ready to say goodbye.

"Would you like to come in?"

"That sounds great," said Zack.

He locked his car and followed Nora down a narrow hall to her apartment.

"I just moved in a few weeks ago so it's still a mess," said Nora as she opened the door and turned on the light.

There were several piles of books on the floor and some pictures that hadn't been hung. "It looks fine," said Zack. He put his arms around her. "I really enjoyed being with you today."

"I did too," she said enjoying the feel of his body against hers.

"I don't want it to end."

Nora looked into Zack's eyes and hesitated.

"What's wrong?"

"I don't know if this is right."

"It feels right to me."

"Yes, but…" After her tryst with Dr. Nederman, Nora had felt like being chaste was the right way to go. Yet she liked Zack and didn't want to push him away.

Zack stepped back. "If you want me to leave I will." He turned and began walking toward the door.

"Wait."

She put her arms around his waist. "Don't leave."

Zack turned and kissed her.

"Could we just cuddle for a while?" said Nora.

"Ahhh… yeah… that would be nice."

"Let's see what's on TV." Nora brought out some wine and they each had a glass.

As they relaxed, on her couch, Zack held her closer. She put her head on his chest and closed her eyes. She stroked his arm slowly then kissed him on the neck. Zack reached under her blouse and let his hand roam up the side of her body. Her skin was soft as silk. There was no turning back for either of them.

Afterwards Nora drew the covers over her breasts. Zack tried to conceal his smile, afraid to let her know just how much he enjoyed her company. She snuggled against his chest. *I wonder how long this is going to last,* he thought. He wanted it to last a long time. He drew her close to him and kissed her gently on the cheek. She put her arms around him and then stretched. Zack felt the gentle curve of her buttocks and the soft slope of her back, now cool in the night air.

———————◆———————

Billy heard the thud of his steps ricocheting off the walls of the dorm as he walked down the long empty hallway of Silverman IV. At first he had hated the silence. When a chair tipped over, the staff rushed to see if there was a fight. When the nurse announced medication time, it was like a sword slicing through his eardrums. But now he appreciated the quiet. He thought about Linda. He had not heard from her in weeks. Was she breaking up with him? Maybe she had lost her phone privileges. He ran her absence over and over in his mind until he had a plan. He would take the problem to Father Meyer and confide in him. That would put him in good stead with the priest and help him find out what was going on with Linda.

Billy checked the door to the counseling office. The door was closed but he heard voices inside. He turned around and walked back down the hall where he passed Craig, the newest arrival to Silverman IV. Billy didn't know much about him except that he walked from one end of the unit to the other, swinging his arms and taking long strides. He told Billy that he needed to walk ten miles a day. He paced off the unit and determined that it was 250 feet long. That meant he would have to walk 211 lengths to reach his goal. The other patients generally stayed out of his way and the staff didn't interfere. There were worse things one could do to fill one's time Billy figured. It didn't seem to interfere with any other activities. Not that there were any. The unit was still locked down.

Billy went back to the couseling office where Calvin, a burly man with a short red crew cut, was just leaving. He was carrying a Bible and Billy heard him say, "Thank you Father. I'll try and pray more and hope that the devils will leave me alone long enough to begin working on my behavior."

"That's fine, my son," said Father Meyer. "God be with you."

Calvin looked at Billy on the way out, letting his eyes linger.

"I wish he wouldn't look at me like that," Billy said to Father Meyer after Calvin was out of ear shot.

"Oh, Calvin means well," said Father Meyer. "He just needs to trust in the Lord and he'll be fine." He gently put his arm around Billy's back. "Come in, Billy. I hope you are doing better."

Billy sat in the chair he always sat in, a red chair with cushions now faded and tattered in spots. He looked at a poster Father Meyer had recently put on the wall of an ant walking up the side of a tree carrying a huge leaf, many times its size. It read, *"The Lord helps those who help themselves."*

Billy grinned. "I like your poster."

"Yes, I couldn't resist buying it," said Father Meyer, glancing at it before he sat down. "What does it say to you?"

"Let me think," said Billy. "I guess we've all got to learn to carry more of our burdens." He was quiet for a moment.

"And what are your burdens, Billy?"

Billy looked at the floor. "I have been hurting, Father," he began. "I have this girlfriend... or I had this girlfriend... I don't know. I haven't heard from her for weeks and I'm afraid I won't see her again. We were really close... and suddenly I don't know what happened."

"And what's this girl's name?" asked Father Meyer, leaning forward in his chair.

"Linda. Her name is Linda," Billy said, looking up. A wave of sadness came over him. It surprised him because he hadn't intended to share any emotion with the priest. He had only wanted to make believe he was letting Father Meyer penetrate his protective shell. He tried to blink his tears away then lowered his head so Father Meyer wouldn't notice.

"I'm sorry to hear that, Billy," said Father Meyer, his voice becoming soft and warm. "Have you tried to contact her?"

Billy took a deep breath and raised his head. "I've been trying to get in touch with her for a couple weeks now. I hope nothing has happened to her."

"Where does she live?"

"She lives here."

"Here?"

"Yes. She's a patient over at New Horizons. I've tried calling over there but they tell me she can't receive any calls so I don't know what's going on." He paused. "I… I don't know if you can do this but… Never mind."

"What is it?"

"I don't want to get you in trouble."

Father Meyer smiled. "Why don't you tell me what it is and we'll see if there is a problem."

"I just want to know if Linda's all right. Maybe you could just check on her for me."

"Well, I think I can manage that."

"She's been the only thing keeping me going all this time and I was looking forward to seeing her. I met her at a dance and we hit it off pretty good."

"I don't want to interfere with her treatment program, but I'll do what I can," said Father Meyer.

◆

Zack was about to pour a cup of coffee but the pot was empty. "Shit," he muttered. "Why can't the fucking p.m. shift ever remember to make coffee?"

Silverman IV was quiet except for the sounds of snoring. Zack dumped out the stale coffee, scooped fresh grounds into the strainer then filled the water reservoir. He flipped the switch on the aging machine and soon the smell of fresh coffee filled the air. He hated working two night-shifts and three P.M.'s each week. His sleep cycle was being constantly disrupted and he had to drown himself with coffee just to stay awake. When he finished working his two night shifts and wanted to go to bed at a normal hour, he had trouble sleeping. Now he was hooked on prescription sleeping pills. When his prescription ran out, he had begun lifting sedatives from the patients' medicine cabinet. His request for a schedule change had been turned down.

Zack sat down and opened the chart of the new arrival, Joshua, a 25-year-old college student from Boise who had been admitted to State Hospital South about a month earlier. Zack turned to the admission notes and began reading:

Patient appears severely depressed after breaking up with girlfriend. He dropped out of school and began stalking her. She reported him to the police. Boise PD issued a restraining order but he continued following her. Patient began to associate with fundamentalist Christian sect and soon began preaching about the sins of the flesh to strangers on the street. When cold weather set in he began sleeping in alleyways and begging for spare change. On 21 October went into a TV store and began smashing television sets with a baseball bat. His parents called SHS and had him committed. When he arrived at Silverman IV he told the staff that Satan was tempting him with scantily clad women on TV and he had to put a stop to it. Initially diagnosed as schizophrenic and is responding well to medication.

As Zack glanced up, he noticed Joshua standing on the other side of the counter. He quickly closed the chart.

"Having trouble sleeping?" asked Zack.

"I just can't stop thinking about Beth."

Zack wasn't supposed to engage in conversation after lights out but the only other person working on the unit was a therapy tech named Charlene who was taking a nap in the back room.

"Was that your girlfriend?"

"We were engaged to be married," said Joshua, smiling broadly. He stared off into the distance, then his smile vanished, and he cast his eyes downward.

"Didn't work out?"

"We were so much in love. I can't figure out why she did it."

"Did what?"

"We wanted to wait so our wedding night would be perfect and we could share the spirit of God between us.

"So…" Zack began but stopped. He didn't want to upset Joshua. He was doing so well on the medications. Suddenly the coffee pot stopped sputtering.

"Be back in a minute," said Zack. "You want a cup?"

"No thanks."

Zack turned and walked into the nurse's station. He poured himself a cup of coffee and returned to the counter where Joshua was resting his head on his folded arms.

"Let's sit down," said Zack. They walked into the dayroom and turned on a light. "So you wanted to wait to have sex until you were married?" It was a simple technique he'd learned from his counseling class called a reflection. It was designed to let the patient know that the counselor understood what he was saying.

"No," said Joshua. "I wanted to have sex with Beth but I knew that Satan had planted the idea in my brain. I prayed to Jesus to cast Satan from my body and he did." Joshua smiled.

"What did you want?" asked Zack. He hadn't anticipated that answer and decided to go back to the beginning.

"I wanted to marry Beth and have lots of children with her and raise them as Christians. I wanted us to be able to worship together as a family. Is that so bad?"

"And what did Beth want?"

Joshua hung his head and ran his fingers through his hair. Zack took a sip of his coffee and waited. Finally Joshua raised his head and looked at Zack. His eyes were red and tears formed in the corners.

"Beth wanted only to walk in the light of Jesus and make her body a vessel for his will," Joshua said, his voice cracking with emotion. "That's what we both wanted." Joshua began to cry. "That's all we wanted, that's all we wanted…"

Zack was afraid he had gone too far. *Maybe another simple reflection.*

"So all you wanted was to become a good Christian couple?"

"Yes, yes. That's all we wanted," said Joshua. Zack handed him a tissue.

"But then something happened," said Zack.

Joshua took a quick breath then began mumbling. To Zack It sounded like a conversation between two entities. One voice was high pitched and mocking in tone while the other was angry. Periodically, Joshua would shake his head and stare up at the ceiling, then go back to looking at the floor, making indecipherable sounds.

"Joshua, Joshua," prodded Zack. "Joshua, what's going on?"

Joshua looked up abruptly. His eyes were fixed on something behind Zack. He began moving his lips again.

He's obviously hallucinating, but who does he think he's talking to—Satan or God or maybe just some sort of spirit? Maybe I should call the night supervisor. No, I'll just wait and see what happens. Zack went to get another cup of coffee. When he returned Joshua had his fly open and was starting to masturbate.

"No, no, you can't do that here," cried Zack.

Joshua just smiled and continued.

"Oh shit, Joshua. Jesus Christ. Take it into the bathroom. Come on," said Zack motioning him to follow.

Joshua wouldn't budge, but he stopped long enough for Zack to make eye contact.

"Come on, Joshua. It's okay. Just do it in the bathroom."

The sounds of their voices woke Carlene who stumbled out of the nurses' station. "What's going on," she said, wiping her eyes.

"You don't want to know," said Zack, but when Carlene looked at Joshua she shook her head and rolled her eyes.

Joshua looked back at Carlene and tucked himself in. Zack led him to the lavatory and closed the door. He went back to the nurses' station where Carlene was pouring herself some coffee. She was short with heavy thighs and a warm smile. She had been working night shift on the unit for two years and had often tried to mother the young men in her charge. She had even given them back rubs when they had trouble sleeping, a practice Zack thought would eventually lead to trouble.

"What's going on?" she asked.

"Joshua couldn't sleep so I decided to talk with him," said Zack.

Carlene put some powdered cream into her coffee and stirred it with a plastic spoon. She was Zack's immediate supervisor and knew that having discussions with patients after lights out was against the rules, but since she had routinely violated that directive many times herself, she let it pass. She walked out of the glassed-in office to the outside desk.

"What were you talking about?"

"Something about his girlfriend... Beth... I think that's what her name was... they were..."

"Wait a minute," said Carlene. "Do you hear a shower?"

The sound of running water was coming from the bathroom.

"It's probably Joshua," said Zack. "I'll check it out."

When he went into the bathroom he saw thick clouds of steam rising from the shower stall. Joshua was standing under a shower with his clothes on. The temperature dial was on high.

When Zack reached in to turn off the faucet he burned his arm. Joshua's skin was bright red.

"What are you doing here?" asked Zack.

Joshua looked up and smiled. His lips were quivering and his eyes were bloodshot. "I'm fighting with Satan."

Carlene came in. "Is everything all right?"

"No, everything is definitely not all right. Joshua scalded himself badly."

Carlene grabbed some towels and they dried Joshua off before calling the night supervisor, who decided to have security transport Joshua to the county hospital in Pocatello. "Write up a report on this," she told Carlene. After she left, Zack and Carlene collaborated on writing the report as the day shift began to arrive.

As Zack drove home, he wondered if he shouldn't have just told Joshua to go back to bed and left it at that. He knew he had violated hospital policy.

15

Talking to God in Laundromats

AS THE SUN ROSE OVER THE MOUNTAINS his drive home, Zack tried to think of more pleasant things. He thought of Nora and replayed their lovemaking over and over in his mind—how she had melted in his arms, how sweet and lovely she smelled, and how good it had felt when he came inside of her. It had been four days since they had been together and he was dying to see her again. Over the past few weeks, he had grown closer to her than he ever expected and now craved her company. Tonight she was coming over for dinner.

When Zack pulled up to his house, Otis, who had been out all night, was waiting for him at the door. Zack changed into some sweats, fed his cat then took off for a run—his newest attempt at resetting his internal clock. He ran down Harrison Street, crossed over the tracks then headed up toward campus. He took a drink from a water fountain, then retraced his route. When he got home he felt better.

Later that day Nora drove over the railroad bridge on her way to dinner at Zack's house. She looked out at the eastside of town, where her father had spent so many years working with the railroad.

She always felt his spirit when she saw the tracks and heard the locomotives traveling back and forth. She thought of Zack and how she had enjoyed his company and their very special night together. She thought she deserved that night because, after all, Kevin and Maria were getting married. *But what if mother's prophecy somehow came true after all? Then it would be even more difficult to break up with Zack.* She had been praying for an answer and now she had it. *Can I actually do this? Please Lord, give me the strength.* She wiped a tear from her cheek.

At six o'clock, Nora arrived.

Zack opened the door. "Welcome to my humble abode."

He gave her a hug. She felt a little stiff.

"How was your day," he said.

"Just fine," she answered, putting her purse on a chair. "I spent the morning shopping with my mother then I helped her hang up some new drapes. She needs something to occupy her mind these days… can't quite bear to clean out Dad's closet yet."

"It will take time," said Zack. "When my mother died. I couldn't focus on anything for a long time."

"What did she die from?"

"Cancer… it was fairly quick, though."

Nora avoided his eyes. "What is that I smell?"

"You smell a secret home recipe for spaghetti sauce. I hope

you're hungry."

Just then, Otis jumped on the table. ""Scat," said Zack, waving his hand. Otis jumped on the floor and began rubbing against Nora's leg.

She stooped down to pet him. "What a beautiful cat," she said. Otis purred and licked her hand.

After their salad, Zack dished up some spaghetti and sauce then cut up a loaf of Italian bread. He opened a bottle of wine and they ate at the table in the small kitchen. Nora was uncharacteristically quiet. After dinner, she suggested they take a walk. The sun was getting low and the wind was picking up. Zack pulled Nora next to him. She resisted.

"Is something wrong?" asked Zack.

"It's not you. You've been wonderful... I just don't want to..."

"Want to what?"

"I don't want to hurt you. I think we should just be friends."

"Friends?" said Zack, caught off guard. "I thought we were friends."

They crossed a street and walked past a small motel where some Indians were changing a flat tire.

"I enjoyed the other night but sometimes what feels good is not always the right thing to do," said Nora.

"What are you talking about?"

Nora sighed and took Zack's hand.

"I've been avoiding telling you about the vision for a long time."

"The vision? What vision?"

"The vision my mother had."

"What about the vision?"

"It was a vision she had about who I will marry."

Zack stared at her. "Who you will marry?"

"Yes, and I know God wants me to wait for him."

"Wait, let me see if I understand." Zack dropped her hand. "Your mother had a vision of who you are going to marry, so we can't …" he chose his words carefully, "…be together anymore?"

"I'm sorry."

"I can't believe I'm actually hearing this. Your mother actually talks to God and tells you what he says about how you should run your life?" He stared with his mouth open. Women had broken up with him before but at least he had understood why.

"I have a friend named Karen," said Nora gently. "She was living with her boyfriend and they had a baby. They weren't married and they broke up. Now she's a single mother and her child has no father."

"What does that have to do with us?"

"God wants men and women to be together, but he wants them to have a commitment. He wants them to be married. All this playing around is fun for the moment but, in the end, it can only cause pain."

"So is your mother a prophet or something?"

"She doesn't claim to be a prophet, but she does have a special gift from the Holy Spirit."

Zack stared at Nora again. This couldn't be happening, he thought, because it didn't make any sense. Yet, the implication of her words was undeniable. They were to have no more sex. After wanting her for so long and finally having her for one glorious night, she was ending it. There must be something he could say to change her mind.

"So, who are you supposed to marry?"

"You don't know him."

"But you do?"

"Yes, but I'd rather not talk about this anymore." Nora turned around. "I think I'd better go home."

"Does he know he's supposed to marry you?

"The time is not right."

"What if you mother's vision is off a little. How do you know we're not supposed to be together?"

"Please, Zack, I really don't want to talk about this anymore."

"Let me tell you a story," shot back Zack, raising his voice. "We have this patient at the State Hospital who used to talk with God all the time. He used to talk to God in laundromats and walking down the street and having a milk shake at McDonalds. Eventually he began to sit with God. One day, he and God were having lunch together in a restaurant when someone saw this poor man talking to himself and sat down across from him to keep him company. Johnny—that's not his real name—Johnny picked up his steak knife and stabbed the guy because he was taking God away from him."

Nora walked faster. "It isn't like that." Her car was in sight.

"What I'm trying to say is that I thought we felt something for each other. At least, I did. I don't want this idea you have to get between us. There must be another reason you don't want to see me anymore. Maybe you need some more time to think about it."

"I didn't say I didn't want to see you anymore." Nora crossed the street to her car. "I just want to be friends." She unlocked the door.

Zack leaned against it. "Okay, we can be friends." He reached out and gave her a hug.

"Please," said Nora with tears in her eyes, "I have to leave."

Zack took a step forward. She opened the door and slid inside.

As she drove away Zack shook his head. "First time I've ever been dumped by the Holy Ghost."

During their final exam in psych class, Zack glanced over at Nora and sighed. She was on the other side of the classroom with her legs crossed, wearing a short skirt and black pumps. Transfixed, Zack slowly traced the smooth curve of her calves down to the tips of her softly frosted toenails. He pried his eyes off her long enough to look at the test.

The exam was multiple-choice. Zack slowly went over some questions he was unsure of. He wanted Nora to leave before him. That way he wouldn't be tempted to wait for her. Although they had exchanged pleasantries, he still missed her desperately. What could he say to her? That she was crazy? That she was living in a fantasy world? He didn't want to insult her. *People believed what they wanted to believe.* After an hour, Nora turned in her exam. As he watched her leave the room, Zack remembered their first kiss, so warm and tender. It still didn't seem possible that now she was walking out of his life forever. He quickly finished the rest of the exam. Afterward, he went outside, had a cigarette and looked toward the mountains. The Aspen trees were turning yellow-green and the sagebrush was sweetly redolent.

———————◆———————

That Sunday Kevin and Maria were married at the Church of the Holy Spirit. About forty people attended including Maria's parents and several of her uncles from Ecuador. The bride wore a white laced wedding gown. Though they were invited, Nora and her mother chose not to attend.

16

Pummeled Meat

ZACK SNATCHED A BEER OUT OF THE REFRIGERATOR and sat down across from a poster of the jagged Teton Mountain Range.

"Three weeks and five days since Nora and I broke up, but who's counting," he said with a bitter smile. He refocused his eyes on the poster and realized that climbing in the Tetons was another dream he had ignored. But between school and work he hadn't had the time to do it.

"It's time to stop thinking about Nora." He pushed himself out of his armchair, shuffled over to his computer and began searching the Teton National Park website for information on making the climb.

Later that summer, he made the three-hour drive to Jenny Lake, to take the required ropes course. In August, he was ready for the ascent up the stone face of the 14,000 foot Grand Teton peak. The park service assigned him to a party of nine other climbers led by a professional guide.

After an introductory lecture from the guide, they started up an easy grade along a well-worn trail, then hiked along a rocky stream, past a marble canyon. At a rest stop, Zack took off his socks, put adhesive pads on his blisters, and filled up his canteen with glacial melt. Soon after they resumed the hike, Zack's leg muscles began to cramp and he stopped briefly to rub it out. He leaned over with his hands on his knees and inhaled.

"What's wrong?" asked the guide, a bronzed man in shorts with muscular legs.

"It's okay. Just gotta get my breath."

"Why don't you walk in front? We don't want you to get too far back."

"Right."

Zack and the group began the long slow climb, traversing back and forth across the side of the bowl-shaped glacial circ. Zack's sweat ran into his eyes and down his shirt. Then his legs began to cramp again. It started to rain. The wind howled pelting Zack's face with stinging raindrops.

When they reached the lower saddle, Zack was gasping for air. The other hikers passed him. At 4 p.m., they reached the Quonset, a five-foot-high half dome made out of drainage culvert with doors at either end. He ducked his head and entered, then dropped to the floor, panting amidst piles of multicolored sleeping bags and backpacks.

"Here. Have a drink of water," said the guide handing him a plastic jug. "How are you doing?"

"I'll be okay. Just have to rest a little and get used to the thin air."

"Well, have a good rest. You'll need it tomorrow. We'll be getting up early so we can be the first party up there. We don't want anyone kicking rocks down on us."

Zack guzzled down some water and finished the rest of his trail mix. Soon everyone turned their lanterns off and went to sleep. He snuggled into his sleeping bag but quickly broke out in a sweat. He threw off the covers and soon started shivering. He re-covered himself. Then he was thirsty. He located a cup, squeezed some water from a collapsible water bag, and drank. It tasted like plastic and he ran outside to vomit. When he came back, his legs cramped again and he had a splitting headache. At 3 a.m. the guide rousted everybody up. It was still dark outside and the Quonset was creaking in the wind.

Zack tried to get up, but his leg muscles cramped and he rolled to the floor. His worst fears were coming to pass. He would have to endure thirteen agonizing belays to reach the summit and he was afraid he might lose his grip. He looked up at the guide and forced out the words.

"I'm cramping. You guys go up without me."

The guide furrowed his brow "Are you sure?"

"Sure. You go. I'll stay. I don't want to slow you down."

Zack was angry and disappointed. It was the end of a dream.

The party left and Zack dozed a while, then fixed himself some hot chocolate and managed not to throw up. He wondered if he could have made the climb after all. *Surely the others were tired, but they didn't quit. Why had I?* He threw his gear into his pack and started down.

Dark clouds moved in and it began to rain. As he got lower it became easier to breathe, but now the back of his thighs felt like pummeled meat. About an hour from the bottom, Zack was surprised when the other hikers from his party started passing him on their way down. *How could they have done it that quickly? If I had stuck with them, maybe I could have made it too.* His mind went numb. He was just glad it was over.

After he returned to the Starchief, he started the engine and turned on the heater. Soon warm air began pouring out through the vents soothing, his battered body.

On the way home, he remembered the good times at the hot springs with Nora. He had hoped that the trip to the Tetons would help him forget her, but instead he felt a deep body hunger to be close to her. He wondered if he should have tried harder to keep her from driving away. His loss of Nora and his weakness on the mountain made him feel like a failure. He turned on the radio but there was only static. His mind drifted. About half way back, he had to slap himself in the face to stay awake.

———————◆———————

In the fall, Zack began attending school full-time. One of his classes was an introductory course in Adlerian Therapy, a technique that emphasized self-analysis through early recollections as well as the order of birth. Students were encouraged to find a partner and begin working with their own memories.

Zack teamed up with a grey haired man with a twinkle in his eyes who turned out to be the campus minister, Reverend Timothy Oakley. Two weeks later, they met at the Student Union to work on a class assignment. Zack was looking over the material when Rev. Oakley sat down on a lounge chair across from him. He was dressed in jeans and a sweater. Zack looked up and smiled.

"How's it going, Reverend Oakley?"

Rev. Oakley grimaced. "You don't have to call me reverend, you know. Tim would be just fine."

"Then Tim it will be," said Zack with a smile. "I feel more comfortable with that anyway."

"I'm just a humble student like everyone else."

"I've been wondering why you're taking this course. Don't you already have a degree in divinity or something?"

"Oh no, I have a BA in psychology and was ordained in the

Unitarian Church, but I'd like to get a masters in counseling."

Zack leaned back in his chair and crossed his legs.

"It gives me more options," Tim added.

Zack raised his eyebrows, "More options?"

"Well, let's just say this is a rather conservative campus and I've had some run-ins with the administration."

"Ah ha. So you might need a counseling degree, in case you need to go into private practice?"

"Something like that," said Tim, reaching into his pocket. "Cigarette?"

"Sure, thanks."

Zack lit it, took a draw, and glanced at his notebook. "You ready to get started?"

"Ready."

Zack leaned forward. "So, tell me about something that affected you in your childhood."

———————◆———————

If discomfort is the measure of effective therapy, Zack was about to get his money's worth. Instead of just studying about group therapy, everyone who signed up for the course automatically became a part of an actual group where members worked with real problems. The group had ten members including the facilitator, a young Ph.D. candidate, and his female assistant.

During the first session, everyone introduced themselves. Zack had trouble keeping his eyes off Margaret, a young divorcee from Chicago. She had big beautiful eyes, brown hair that spilled over her shoulders and a smile that melted Zack's heart. Unlike Nora, she didn't wear any make-up. She didn't need it. She gave Zack a couple of smiles and he smiled back.

As they were leaving class, Zack walked up to her. "So you're from Chicago," he said. "I used to drive a cab there."

"Really," said Margaret. "Are you from there, too?"

"No, I'd been going to school in Madison—the University of Wisconsin. My brother lived in Chicago and I was staying with him one summer."

"I've been to Madison a couple of times. It seemed like a great city."

"Yeah, it was a nice place, but I always wanted to live out west, near the mountains. I just returned from a hike in the Tetons," said Zack.

Margaret's eyes widened and her face broke into a smile. "Oh, that's what I have always wanted to do." Suddenly she cast her eyes down and a worried look came over her face. Zack was afraid he had said something to upset her.

They walked out of the building together. There was a hint of fall in the air as a cool breeze fluttered through the needles of a blue spruce next to the building.

"I'd like to stay and talk but I have to go to work," said Zack. "I'll see you in class next week."

Zack began walking to his car.

"Where do you work?" called out Margaret.

"State hospital in Blackfoot," said Zack over his shoulder. "See you later."

Dr. Nederman leaned back in his chair, clasped his hands behind his neck, and stretched. It was late afternoon and he was revising his lecture notes. The phone rang.

"Excuse me," said his new secretary. "I know you didn't want to be disturbed, but it's Dr. Jackson. He said it was important."

"That's okay," said Dr. Nederman. "I'll always take a call from my boss."

"Hi Tom," said Dr. Jackson. "Hate to disturb you."

"That's okay, Jack. What's up?"

"I'd like to talk to you about something. Do you have time to stop by now?"

"Sure thing," said Dr. Nederman. "I've just got to finish up and I'll be right in." He hung up and wondered what was going on. Jackson usually stopped in his office to talk with him. They had been friends and colleagues for a long time. He took a short walk down the hall to Jackson's office.

"Have a chair," said Dr. Jackson, leafing through a report. "We have a little problem here." Jackson had a full black mustache curled at the ends that reminded Nederman of Wyatt Earp.

"What's up?"

Dr. Jackson looked at Nederman then back down at the papers. "I've just received a formal complaint against you from the Affirmative Action Office... seems a female student is claiming that you sexually harassed her." He handed the report to Dr. Nederman.

Nederman examined it and shook his head. "You know, you try to help someone and this is what happens. No good deed goes unpunished."

"So you remember Beverly Wilson?"

"She was a very troubled person," said Dr. Nederman. "I tried to help her through a difficult period in her life but..."

Dr. Jackson held up his hand and shook his head. "I don't need to know the details now. The Affirmative Action Office wants to hold a formal hearing in ten days and you can give them your side of the story."

"It's nothing," said Dr. Nederman.

"I hope for your sake it is. This isn't the first time," said Dr. Jackson.

"I know, but it's nothing, really," Dr. Nederman said, getting up. "Thanks for letting me know about this."

Dr. Jackson leaned forward. "You know Beverly has left the program don't you?"

Dr. Nederman smiled sadly. "No, I hadn't heard. I'm sorry. I could have helped her."

Wednesday afternoon, as Nora was looking for a place to sit in the cafeteria, Susan Decker from the Clerical Workers Union waved her over.

"I have an interesting piece of gossip for you," said Susan.

Nora sat across from Susan and un-wrapped the tuna sandwich she'd brought from home. She was sick of cafeteria food but liked the bright open space after being cooped up in the office all morning.

"Gossip for me?" said Nora.

"Yes. It's about your old boss, Dr. Nederman."

Nora could feel her muscles tighten as her body went on defense.

"I really don't have a thing to do with him anymore," said Nora.

"Remember I told you he got caught a few years ago making inappropriate moves on his secretary?"

"Oh yeah, I seem to remember something about that."

"He did it again."

Nora pictured her replacement. For a minute she felt insulted. How could Nederman have such poor taste?

"He was messing around with the new secretary? I wouldn't have thought he'd try something with... what's her name?"

"No. No, it's a graduate student this time. Her name is Beverly Wilson. She filed a complaint against him with Affirmative Action. Claimed he fondled her. They're having a hearing about it a week from Friday."

"Oh. Well, that's too bad," said Nora. "I mean it's good that someone filed a complaint." Nora took a bite of her sandwich and began to feel sick. *Why hadn't she filed a complaint? Why had she let Nederman get away with it?*

She put the sandwich down and took a sip of coffee.

"I hope they really burn him," said Susan. "He deserves it. I just thought you'd want to know." She got up.

"Thanks for letting me know, Susan," said Nora. "Have a good day."

◆

As Nora drove to her mother's house to check up on her, she thought of Dr. Nederman's hands on her body. She began to feel sick and took a deep breath. *I can't keep this inside anymore.*

When she arrived home, she told her mother about her affair with Dr. Nederman. Her mother listened quietly.

When Nora was finished, she hung her head and began crying softly. Her mother drew her close and stroked her hair. Nora pushed away and found a Kleenex.

She asked her mother a question that she already knew the answer to. "How long must I wait?"

"I can't tell you that, dear," said her mother. "But I do know that our faith is being tested by Satan. Don't you see? God has chosen me to reveal his plan for you, and Satan is trying to tear you away from me. You must realize that he will be merciless in his efforts."

"But, mother, I'm so tired of waiting. Kevin is married. Can't you see that he's found someone else?"

"We can't know the mind of God. All we can do is to try and live by His word." Nora's mother put her arms around her daughter and whispered, "It's not easy being a Christian."

17

Tomorrow Never Comes

ZACK HURRIED DOWN THE LONG HALL ON SILVERMAN IV. Each month, the staff met to discuss three patients and make treatment recommendations. Normally, Zack enjoyed brainstorming sessions. But today he was trying to figure out how to cover his ass in the Joshua Taylor scalding incident. He knew that if he had followed unit procedure and escorted Joshua back to his room, it wouldn't have happened. Or would it? Maybe Joshua would have taken the shower anyway. Carlene had been the shift lead, but she was sleeping when it happened and Zack didn't want to rat on her. He was prepared to take the blame.

Zack entered the unit psychologist's office as the meeting began. His attention drifted in and out until Marla, the head nurse, picked up Joshua's grey metal chart and began reading.

"Joshua Taylor, 25, admitted to Silverman IV 6/6/96, diagnosis: schizophrenic." She leafed through the nurses notes from Pocatello Regional Medical Center then shook her head. "He had second degree burns to his scalp and had to be heavily sedated. I see we've changed the medications too."

"I was there the night it happened," said Zack. He stopped and chose his words carefully. "He was up late and we were talking about his girlfriend and how he wanted to marry her and be a good Christian, when suddenly he began hallucinating. Then he started masturbating. I took him to the bathroom and closed the door. Next thing I knew, he's scalding himself under the shower. Said he was trying to burn Satan out of his body."

"How's he doing now?" asked Marla.

"He's doing better," Zack began. "No hallucinations. The skin is flaking off his scalp and we're applying lotion three times a day. It will take a while until he's fully healed."

"We'll continue to monitor him and hopefully get him stabilized on medications, so we can get him into a residential treatment facility." said Marla. She looked around. "Is there anything more? Okay, thanks for coming. Zack, I'd like to talk with you."

After everyone had left, Marla closed the door. "Have a seat Zack. This won't take long."

Zack took a deep breath and braced himself. He knew what was coming.

"You know I'm not a stickler with rules," Marla began. "But you shouldn't have been talking with patients in the middle of the night. It can lead to problems, as you found out. I'm going to give you a warning, but if it happens again, I'll have to write you up."

"Sorry," said Zack. "I just wanted to help him out."

Marla got up, opened the door to leave then glanced over her shoulder. "The road to hell is paved with good intentions."

◆

Zack was in the cafeteria at ISU, grabbing a bite between classes, when he noticed a distinguished looking minister in a black suit with a white collar walking toward his table smiling. It was Tim Oakley from counseling class.

"How are you doing, Zack? Mind if I join you?"

"No, not at all," said Zack, grinning. "At first I didn't recognize you. It's not every day that a man of the cloth asks to share a table with a heathen like me."

"Oh well, don't be too hard on yourself, we're all sinners you know," said Tim, lighting a cigarette. He took a drag, leaned back into the corner of the booth, and glanced toward the plethora of similarly clad clergymen emerging from the hallway.

Zack's mouth dropped. "My God, we're being invaded."

"Don't worry, it's just a lunch break," said Tim, waving to some members of the group. "We're having a meeting of the Intermountain Campus Fellowship Association, and I'm giving a seminar."

"Congratulations," said Zack. "What's the subject?"

Rev. Oakley adjusted his glasses and tipped the end of his cigarette in the ashtray.

"It's called, 'Tomorrow Never Comes.'"

Zack laughed, "Great title, but what does it mean?"

"One thing most prophecies have in common is that they rarely come to pass. It's a lot easier to say that an event was prophesized after it occurred," said Tim.

"If they don't come true, then why do people believe in them?" asked Zack.

"Ah, that's the sixty-four thousand dollar question. Basically it's because they want to. We live in a scary and unpredictable world. Charismatic leaders have found that prophesy is a powerful tool to control the faithful. There have been some interesting studies done by social scientists on that very point. I just finished reading an article about failed prophecies. They found that after a failed prophecy, the one who made the false prediction would often tell the faithful that it was just a test of faith or that the event predicted actually occurred but on a spiritual plane. Faith is a powerful motivator but it can be abused like anything else."

Zack noticed Nora coming through the cafeteria line with a tray. His heart skipped a beat. She saw him, smiled and walked over to the table.

"How are you, Zack? I hope I'm not interrupting anything."

"No, not at all. Have a seat."

Zack scooted over and Nora slid in next to him. He had not been this close to her in weeks and warmed to her presence.

"It's good to see you again," said Zack giving her a little hug.

Nora blushed, avoiding his gaze.

"Nora, this is Reverend Tim Oakley from the Campus Ministry."

"Pleased to meet you," said Tim, crushing out his cigarette. He stared at Nora just long enough to make her uncomfortable, then smiled. "I didn't realize that Zack had such a refined taste in women."

Nora blushed. "I've seen you around, Reverend Oakley, but I don't think we ever met."

Tim beamed at Nora. "Well, then its past due."

"Reverend Oakley is giving a seminar at the campus ministry meeting about false prophesy."

"Oh really," said Nora, taking a bowl of salad off her tray.

The smell of her perfume rekindled Zack's desire.

"What sort of false prophets are you talking about?" she asked.

"Oh, there are all kinds," began Tim. "But the prophets I'm concerned with are the ones that manipulate others with false predictions. If God wants to talk with someone, he won't go to someone else. He will talk to them directly, through their heart."

"You don't think God communicates with people who have a special relationship with Him?" said Nora. She stripped the paper wrapping from her straw, put the straw in her drink and took a sip.

Zack stared as her full, red lips left a small smudge of lipstick on the straw.

"I don't know the mind of God," said Tim. "But—"

"We should never try to guess what is in the mind of God," Nora said quickly.

"Very often, people will try and comfort others with their interpretation of God's will, but these words are not a replacement for what a person feels deep in their soul. We sometimes call it intuition. It's an internal validation of our life."

Nora stared into her salad, where little pieces of bacon sprinkled on the lettuce had fallen into the bottom of the bowl and lay there next to shards of onion and carrots.

"I… ah… I… was just thinking," Nora stammered. She took a quick breath and stopped. *I want to believe that mother's prophecy will come to pass, but now I'm not so sure. And what of Zack? I feel something for him, but I turned away his affections, then I defiled myself with Dr. Nederman. Whatever will I do?*

Zack watched Nora closely and realized that she was struggling for words. He was about to come to the rescue, but stopped.

Tim glanced up at Zack and winked.

"Nothing wrong with that," said the Reverend Oakley. "That's what God gave us a brain for."

Nora looked at her watch. "Oh my, I should be heading back to work now." She stabbed a piece of lettuce and put it in her mouth before pushing the salad bowl away and getting up. Suddenly the room began to spin and she leaned forward on the table.

"Are you all right?" asked Zack.

"I think so," said Nora, taking a deep breath. "I just felt a little dizzy there, for a second."

"Why don't you sit back down," said Reverend Oakley. "You look a little pale."

"No, I'll be fine."

Zack gently placed his hand on her shoulder. Nora smiled, "I feel better now. Maybe I'm coming down with something."

"I hope you will be all right. It was very nice meeting you," said Tim, gently taking Nora's hand.

"Good luck on your speech," said Nora. "It was very... interesting talking with you."

---◆---

The Affirmative Action Grievance Committee met in a conference room at the campus library. The committee chair, Dr. Shelton, a middle aged black man with graying hair, called the meeting to order.

He turned to his assistant, who was sitting next to him.

"Could you please let Dr. Nederman know that we are ready?"

The young woman left and came back with Dr. Thomas Nederman

and a heavy-set man with a beard.

Nederman took a seat and looked around the room. "This is Professor Stevens," he told the committee.

"Welcome Professor Stevens," said Mr. Shelton. "Are you here as a witness?"

"No. I'm here to ah… observe… I guess."

Nederman recognized most of the committee members. Each of them had a stack of papers containing reports of the initial investigation, copies of official policies, and statements of the principles.

Beverly Wilson was sitting at the end of a long table with a woman in a business suit who Nederman assumed was her counsel. Beverly looked so different, he thought. Her long golden hair was cut short and she was wearing a blouse with high collar. She avoided eye contact with him. Nederman shifted nervously in his seat.

Chairman Shelton looked around and turned to his assistant. "Laura, you can turn on the tape recorder. I think we're ready to begin. I want to welcome everyone today and remind you that this is not a court of law and formal rules of evidence do not apply. We will not make a decision until we have had a chance to listen and ask questions of each party in this dispute. Ms. Wilson has chosen to bypass the informal hearing phase of the process, so I hope everyone has had time to review the documents." He looked around the room. "I want to impress on everyone that everything that's said here is confidential. After this hearing the committee will meet within ten days to make recommendations for action to President Cole."

Chairman Shelton looked at Beverly Wilson. "I understand that you have withdrawn from the MA Counseling program. I'm sorry to hear that. Did this incident have anything to do with that decision?"

"Yes it did," said Beverly. She cast her eyes downward, shuffled the pile of papers in front of her, then shot a quick glance toward Nederman. "I felt that I could no longer continue in this program… under the circumstances." She paused and bit her lip. "Dr. Nederman was my sponsor. I trusted him."

"But surely you can find another sponsor," said Shelton.

Susan Decker, the union rep, intervened. "I think what she's trying to say is that Dr. Nederman has created an environment that is hostile to an atmosphere of learning. Excuse me for speaking for you but isn't that true, Beverly?"

"Yes, thank you. I had heard rumors that Dr. Nederman had been… " She paused. "…a little too friendly with some of his female students, but he was a perfect gentleman to me, at least in the beginning. I needed a sponsor, so we began working together."

"Excuse me," interrupted a man in a tweed sport coat. "Did working together include massages?"

"I came in one day with a headache and he offered me a neck rub. I said okay. That was it."

"So, you thought that was as far as it would go."

"Yes. I trusted him."

"Then what's this about being fondled?"

"A week later, we were in his office. We were going over some counseling tapes... ah... tapes of me counseling a client... that I brought in and he offered to give me another massage. I was a little hesitant, but he insisted."

"You felt compelled to give him permission?" asked Sue Decker.

"He was my advisor. I didn't want him to think... you know... that I thought that he was doing anything wrong," said Beverly.

Chairman Shelton leaned forward. "Then what happened?"

Beverly took a deep breath. "He put on some music and told me to relax. He started massaging my neck."

"You were sitting in the beanbag chair?"

"Yes, he was kneeling down in back of me. I tried to relax. He began massaging my shoulders. The next thing I knew, he had his hand on my breast. I sat up and didn't know what to say."

"How did you feel?" asked a woman with wire rimmed glasses.

"I was shocked."

"Did you say anything?"

"He acted like nothing happened."

"What did you do?"

"I left."

"You didn't say anything?"

"I told him I had to leave. I grabbed my tape recorder and left."

The chairman turned to Dr. Nederman. "Is that what happened?"

Nederman smiled and shook his head. "I'm sorry Beverly misinterpreted our interaction. I was only trying to help her relax. She had been under a lot of pressure to complete her assignment before the end of the semester and I wanted to let her know that I was there to help."

"So you don't deny that you gave her a massage?"

"No, no. I offer it to all my students. It's part of the body psychotherapy technique pioneered by Dr. Wilhelm Reich."

"Does that include grabbing someone's breast?" asked the woman with the wire rimmed glasses.

"Oh, no. I didn't grab her breast."

"She said you did."

"I know, but I'm afraid she was mistaken."

"Why would Beverly withdraw from a program because she was mistaken?"

"She was under pressure."

The room was silent for a moment. Beverly began to cry softly. Her counsel handed her tissue and she wiped her eyes.

"I withdrew because I hated how I felt," she said, regaining her composure. "After I got home, I started thinking about it and realized that I couldn't continue in a program where such behavior was tolerated. Then I became angry. I have wanted to help people with problems all my life and this is what I get? I know it's his word against mine, but I just wanted to let you know what type of predator you have in your midst."

Nederman looked down at the table, shaking his head from side to side.

The chairman looked around the room. "Are there any more questions or comments?" Dr. Shelton waited briefly, and seeing none, softly said, "I want to thank everyone for coming today. The committee will meet next Wednesday in closed session. This meeting is adjourned."

Dr. Nederman hurried out of the meeting room, his shirt soaked with sweat.

18

Doubting Thomas

JOSHUA TAYLOR SAT AT A STEEL TABLE across from Billy Butts and another patient playing a game of Risk. Zack watched the players. Billy was recklessly aggressive and tried to amass as many troops on the borders before launching a head-on assault into enemy territory. The other player was more thoughtful and tried to form an alliance with Joshua to whittle away at Billy's forces and avoid a devastating assault. Joshua played both sides against each other and won. Zack congratulated him.

Joshua smiled. "That was one of my favorite games when I was a kid. I would play with my dad. At first he would let me win, but after I got better, we would battle as if it was real. It was a good way to work out frustrations."

"Better than trying to hold anger in all the time," said Zack. "I'm glad to see that you're doing better… I mean in the game and on the unit."

"I feel a lot better," said Joshua. "No more voices."

"That's great," said Zack. Short responses were part of the treatment plan until Joshua had more individual counseling.

That night they had a dance on the unit. The patients cleared the tables and chairs from the dining area, and the kitchen staff brought refreshments. At eight o'clock, the young women started arriving from other units along with their staff escorts.

The first woman to arrive was Billy's girlfriend, Linda. She had been on restriction, but Father Meyer had pulled some strings to get her off her unit.

"Welcome to Silverman IV," said Leo, a burly therapy tech with a beard and a baritone voice.

Linda looked at Leo with wide eyes and said nothing.

"Come on in. I won't bite," he said with a laugh.

Linda edged her way around Leo and headed toward the refreshments.

Her stringy long hair was plastered to the side of her head and her sneakers had holes on the top. Her tee shirt read "*Yippy, Yippy, Fuck*" in letters so worn that they were barely legible.

Billy stepped forward and said in a deep voice, "How ya doing."

"Where's the fuckin' drinks," said Linda. "The fuckin' meds are drying out my mouth and if I don't get something I'm gonna lose it."

Billy rolled his head and answered in a monotone, "Over here." He led her to the punch bowl and handed her a paper cup. "Hey," he said to Leo. "Do you think we could get some music going here?"

"Sure thing," said Leo. "Perhaps a little disco?"

"I like disco," came a voice. Leo turned around and saw Frank Nelson, a normally disheveled schizophrenic, dressed in slacks and a colorful shirt with a collar. His hair was neatly combed and his leather shoes were shined to a fine finish.

"You look great tonight Frank," said Leo.

"Thank you," said Frank. "You are looking very well yourself."

Good Lord, thought Leo. *Is this really the Frank Nelson whose speech resembles word salads and has an affinity for masturbating in front of female staff?*

Leo put on a disco tape. Frank slowly started rotating his hips and rolling his shoulders with a natural rhythm. More women arrived. A couple of the young women were standing around looking lost. Frank approached one of them who wore heavy make-up and a pink dress and asked her to dance.

She gave Frank the once over and said, "No, maybe later." Frank asked the woman next to her who accepted. She was tall and thin and they danced well together, matching each other's moves. Other couples joined them and soon the party was rolling. After the pizza arrived, some of the dancers took a break to eat.

Joshua inched his way out of his room, hesitated, then walked slowly down the hall. As he passed the young woman in the pink dress, she looked him over and put out her hand.

"Hello, my name is Sheila."

"Hi," said Joshua slowly taking her hand. "I'm Joshua."

"Do you want to dance?" asked Sheila.

Joshua glanced at the dance floor then back at Sheila.

He recalled he had once believed that dancing was a sin.

He smiled sheepishly. "It's been a while."

"Come on, I'll show you how." Sheila took Joshua's hand and led him to the dance floor. "Just move your body with the music like this," she said, beginning to sway side to side and clap her hands.

Joshua listened to the music then slowly started moving from side to side. Sheila took both his hands and began swinging them to the rhythm of the music.

Leo and Zack stood off to the side. "I think everyone is having a good time," said Leo.

"Yes, I think so, too," said Zack, scanning the crowd. "Wait a minute, someone is missing. Where is Billy and his girlfriend?

Leo looked down the hallway. "I don't see them." They looked at each other quickly.

"You take the north wing and I'll take the south," said Zack. He hurried down the hall to the shower room and went in. There were two people in one of the toilet stalls. When Zack opened the door, Billy had his pants down facing Linda who was sitting on the toilet.

"Okay, that's it," said Zack. "Put on your pants."

"Hey asshole, get the fuck out of here," said Linda. "Can't you see we're having a good time?"

"Zip it up, Billy," said Zack.

Billy hesitated. "Be out in a minute."

"Now!" Zack raised his voice.

"Hey, I could do you both," said Linda.

Zack looked at her in disgust and shook his head. "You too."

Zack led them back to the party and found an escort to return Linda to her unit. Billy spent the rest of the night brooding in a corner.

In late September, Zack decided he needed a break from Silverman IV and used some of his vacation time. He invited Margaret from his group therapy class to join him for a weekend of backpacking in the Sawtooth Mountain wilderness of central Idaho. She jumped at the chance.

Zack picked Margaret up early Saturday morning. She was all smiles. They grabbed some coffee at a convenience store, gassed up then, began driving across the barren plain. The Sawtooth Mountains were 150 miles northwest of Blackfoot on the other side of the Snake River.

"Have you spent much time in the mountains?" Zack asked.

"No…I…always wanted to, but Ernie never asked me…" said

Margaret.

"Ernie. That would be your ex?"

"We came out to Idaho together but... I don't know... you probably don't want to hear about this."

"I'm all ears. After all, we're going to be counselors, right?"

"I guess so. Well, Ernie never wanted to take me camping with him. He always said he needed time to be alone. After a while, I began to feel like he was rejecting me but, well, I kind of thought I deserved it."

"Why's that?"

Margaret was silent for a while.

"After we were married, I became pregnant. We didn't have much money and I wanted to go to grad school. Ernie was just starting out as a salesman and working overtime to build up accounts. We're both Catholic and didn't believe in abortion. So after going through a lot of torment, we decided to put the baby up for adoption."

"That must have been tough."

"The church was going to help us find the baby a good home until Ernie changed his mind and wanted us to keep it. I was at the end of my first trimester and knew that I wasn't ready to have a baby so I... I..." When Margaret spoke her voice sounded dead. "I terminated the pregnancy."

"You did what you thought was right," Zack said quickly.

"No, it wasn't right. Nothing about it was right."

Zack tried to think of something to say but came up short.

Margaret stared out the window. "It was very hard on both of us," she said softly. "When I was accepted to grad school at ISU, I hoped we could put the past behind us." She blinked back some tears.

Now Zack understood why, after class, she had cast her eyes downward when he first mentioned he was going hiking in the Tetons.

"I'm sorry you're still hurting but I'm glad you told me." Zack reached over and put his hand on hers.

"I'll be all right." Margaret wiped her eyes.

The road began to climb. They drove north through Sun Valley, then up twenty miles of winding road until they reached the Galena Pass. At the top was a spectacular view of the Sawtooth Range. The jagged mountains were set in a long north-south line and really did look like the teeth on a saw blade.

They stopped the car and took some pictures, then descended down the other side to the floor of a valley. They arrived at Redfish Lake located at the north end of the valley around noon, then took a launch to the other end. From the drop off point, they hiked up a narrow river valley then began a steep ascent. The path switched back and forth through fields of bright yellow and purple asters, their colors striking in the cool thinning mountain air. About mid-afternoon, they stopped at a waterfall to cool off.

Zack shed his pack and helped Margaret to unload hers. "My feet are killing me," he said.

"Mine too," sighed Margaret. She walked to the falls and slapped some water on her face, then cradled her hands and took a drink.

Zack took off his boots and sat on a boulder, dangling his feet in the pond. Margaret did the same. As the sun began getting lower in the sky Zack said, "Rest time is over. Let's go."

When he helped Margaret off the rock, she slid off right into his arms. Zack held her close, wrapping his arms around her warm body.

"Thank you for inviting me on this trip," she said.

Zack turned and kissed her forehead. "Thanks for coming."

They put their shoes back on and then their packs. They were almost out of water, so they filled their canteens before leaving. After a couple more hours hiking they reached Priest Lake. They spent the night there in Zack's pup tent. It was cold and they snuggled together for warmth in their sleeping bags.

In the morning, Zack awoke with his arms around Margaret. He checked his watch and it was 8:45 am. She was still sleeping and sunlight was showing through the tent. Zack decided not to wake her up so he could savor the moment. He had missed sleeping with a woman. Sometimes he woke up with a craving in his body. He remembered a song by Richie Havens— *how did it go? Something about feeling like a motherless child?* He felt comforted to be lying next to Margaret this morning.

Zack carefully pushed himself up and started a fire. Margaret woke up shortly afterward, found a rock in the sun, and sat down.

"How did you sleep?" she asked Zack.

"I slept very well," said Zack, rubbing his hands together. "It's just the getting up that's hard, how 'bout you."

Margaret smiled. "I had a dream about you, about us."

"Really."

Margaret took a deep breath and looked reluctantly toward the fire. Steam was coming from the pot.

"I'd better get the coffee," she said.

Zack found two metal cups and filled them with the boiling water. Margaret stirred in a packet of instant coffee.

"Be careful. It's hot," she warned.

Zack took a sip, and looked over at Margaret. She looked sad. "So, are you going to tell me what was in the dream?"

"I was in my house listening to some music. I think it was Joni Mitchell. Then, I heard someone knocking at my screen door. It was you. I think we had some kind of plans, I'm not sure, but anyway, I couldn't get it to open. I tried to talk to you, but you couldn't hear me. Finally you turned and walked away—like you thought I wasn't there. But I was."

Zack tried to think of something to say. There were many facets to the dream: something to do with fear of rejection, with Ernie, or maybe reluctance to get involved. The house was her body. The door was her chance to interact. She deserved a reply.

He walked over to her. "Knock, knock."

"Who's there?"

"Zack."

"Zack who?"

"Zackadoodle doo," he said with a big smile.

They both started laughing. Zack reached out his arms and she came to him. They stood there in the forest embracing for a moment. Zack leaned down to give her a kiss and she met him half way. They started laughing again.

"How about some breakfast," said Margaret. "Do you like scrambled eggs and bacon?"

"That sounds great. I'll toast some bread on the fire," said Zack.

About mid-morning, they broke camp and headed for the Cramer Lakes, on the other side of the 8,000 foot summit. They hiked up through the scrub pines then above the timber line. On the other side, the three Cramer Lakes stretched out in a line. They scurried down the rocky wall to the first lake and rested. The sun was high and Zack was drenched with sweat.

"I don't know about you but I could use a swim," said Zack.

"It looks a little cold for me," said Margaret. "But if you want to take a swim, go ahead."

Zack stripped down to his underwear, climbed onto a rock and dove into the crystal clear lake. The water was so cold that when he hit the surface he could hardly breathe.

"Holy shit is that cold!" he yelled. He turned around and swam like crazy to a rock and pulled himself up. Margaret threw him a towel.

"You don't know what you're missing," he said, dryng his head.

"I think I do," said Margaret, laughing.

Zack stretched out on a warm rock until he stopped shivering, then threw on some clothes and they explored the shoreline. They soon became exhausted because of the high altitude and strenuous hike. That night they slept well.

———————◆———————

The next day Zack went fishing. Each cast of the silver lure that flashed in the sunlight brought back a beautiful pan-sized mountain trout. He handed the rod to Margaret who brought in some more. Their legal limit was five each, but within an hour they had caught sixteen. On the way back to their camp, they bushwhacked through the forest in case a game warden was lurking nearby. That night they shared a feast of trout, some cheese, sourdough bread and coffee beneath a brilliant starlit sky. At bedtime they zipped their sleeping bags together and started kissing, but when Zack tried to make love to her all he could think of was the passionate night he had spent with Nora.

"What's wrong?" asked Margaret.

I guess I'm tired out from the hike," said Zack kissing her on the forehead. "Let's get some rest."

When he turned over, Zack remembered the softness of Nora's body and the aroma of her perfume. He knew it would take a long time to get her out of his mind. He wished it wasn't so.

After breakfast, they realized that they had used up most of the food so they decided to head back down the mountain. They back-tracked over the ridge and down the other side to the valley where they stopped to rest at a river with flat water-smoothed rocks.

They reached Redfish Lake by noon and waited for the launch. The water was warmer and Zack convinced Margaret to take a swim with him. They took off their clothes and dove into the cool crystal clear water. When they heard the boat they hustled out and got dressed. After they reached the lodge, they had a couple beers and sat outside to watch the tourists splash around in a little beach near the docks.

They drove back over the Galena summit, through Sun Valley, and into the Craters of the Moon, where ancient lava flows had reduced the low hills to a valley of jagged rocks with ominous black spires. They enjoyed good music on the radio and shared more stories.

When Zack dropped Margaret off at her little house she, gave him a big kiss and then melted into his arms.

"What a great weekend," he said.

"Yes," said Margaret looking up at him. "I really enjoyed it too. Do you want to come in?"

"I'd like to, but I better not," said Zack. "I have to be on the unit early tomorrow morning and I'm bushed."

Margaret lowered her eyes and looked away. "Okay."

Zack helped her unload her gear, then climbed back into the Starchief. "I'll see you in class next week."

As he drove away, Zack felt good about their trip. They had shared an adventure and grown closer. Now all he had to do was get Nora off his mind.

Nora went to church with her mother on Sunday morning for the first time in two months. As they walked up the steps of the Church of the Holy Spirit, she felt sad that her father couldn't join them. It had made her feel needed when she helped him slowly walk, step by step, up the stairs with his cane. Reverend Miller was in the lobby and greeted them warmly before her mother went to join the choir members. Nora looked around and found a seat near the front. She quickly glanced back to see if Kevin was there. She was glad she didn't see him.

After the opening hymns and announcements Reverend Miller began his sermon about Jesus' Apostle Thomas. The Reverend was a stocky man in his forties from Tennessee who spoke with country twang. He had been pastor for three years after moving to Idaho from Nashville. Nora thought he looked like a television preacher with his immaculately groomed thick black hair and his charcoal grey suit and vest.

"I want to know how many of you have ever doubted the Word of God." He walked across the stage holding his hand up. "Come on. Let's see your hands." He looked around the room and a few hands went up. "Come on," he said again. "I know there must be more of you out there." A few more people raised their hands half-way. "All right, all right," he said, smiling. "Either most of you are keeping it to yourself or my work here is finished and it's time to move on."

Nora smiled nervously because she was beginning to have her doubts but was afraid to raise her hand.

Reverend Miller walked back to his podium. "I want to talk to you today about a man who walked with Jesus and talked with Jesus, but when he was told that Jesus had returned from the dead, he didn't believe it. John in 20:25 says, 'So the other disciples told him, We have seen the Lord! But he (Thomas) said to them, Unless I see the nail marks in his hands and put my finger where the nails were, and put my hand into his side, I will not believe it.'"

Nora felt queasy when she thought about Thomas sticking his fingers into someone's body. She took a deep breath and folded her arms in front of her.

"The truth is that Thomas didn't want to believe it," said Reverend Miller. "Would you? Would you believe that someone you watched die an agonizing death on the cross, a mortal man who was beaten and cut and left for dead would come back and stand before his disciples like nothing ever happened?"

Reverend Miller brought his microphone to the edge of the stage and bent down, speaking in a low voice. "Thomas wasn't being disloyal, he just lacked faith." He got up and walked to the other side of the stage and pointed into the air. "He was asking for proof. Eight days later, Jesus appeared before his disciples again and this time Thomas was with them. John says in 20:26-29 'Though the doors were locked, Jesus came and stood among them and said, Peace be with you. Then he said to Thomas, put your finger here; see my hands. Reach out your hand and put it into my side. Stop doubting and believe: blessed are those who have not seen and yet have believed.'"

"Now I don't know about you, but at that point I would start believing that Jesus had risen from the dead," shouted Reverend Miller. "Glory halleluiah, there are times in my life when I've had similar doubts. When I was going to college I saw a conflict between science and religion. I have been a Doubting Thomas. Now I want you to know that Jesus never appeared before me in person, but He has shown me that He does exist. Every time I see a flower bloom, or a baby born, or the beautiful colors of a sunset, I see the work of His love. Every day, I walk with Jesus and keep Him in my heart. Every day that I have faith in Him I know that He has faith in me. Praised be Jesus."

Reverend Miller bowed his head, the organist began to play "Jesus is a Friend of Mine" and the choir joined in. Nora looked up and saw the presence of Jesus in her mother who was singing and looking radiant for the first time since her father had died.

After the service ended and she was leaving, Nora noticed Kevin up ahead. She slowed down to avoid him but the crowd pushed her closer. She could see that Kevin was talking to someone and Maria was at his side. As Nora passed silently behind him, she glanced toward Maria and then looked away. Did she really see what she thought she saw? She looked again. Nora always thought of Maria as being very slim but now she had a bulge in her tummy. Just then, she caught Maria's eye.

"Nora, it's so nice to see you again," said Maria.

Kevin turned around and smiled. "Hello, Nora."

"Hello," said Nora, trying her best not to stare at Maria's belly.

Kevin's mother gave Maria a hug.

"Have you heard the news Nora? I'm going to be a grandmother."

Nora looked down at Maria's tummy. "Congratulations."

Maria looked up at Kevin and beamed. "And my husband is going to be a father. We don't know when the baby shower is going to be but we'll send you and your mother an invitation."

"Thank you," said Nora. "I have to go now, goodbye."

As Nora walked toward the choir, she told herself that the birth of a child should be a wonderful thing. Didn't Rev. Miller say it was a sign of the Lord's presence? But it wasn't supposed to happen that way. She and Kevin were supposed to be together, not Maria. It was supposed to be their child. Lost in thought, Nora walked blindly into a potted palm, spilling black dirt all over the rug.

"Oh my," cried her mother who rushed over and righted the palm. "Are you all right?"

"Yes... no... Mother, we need to talk. I just saw Kevin and Maria. She's pregnant," said Nora, as they began walking toward the exit. For a split second her mother looked confused, then she smiled.

"Oh no, Nora, I saw her too. She was just wearing a dress that was a little full in the waist. Don't you think the choir did a fine job this morning? We have another practice scheduled for—"

"Kevin's mother was there. She said she was going to be a grandmother."

"Well, dear, Kevin has sisters, too. It was probably one of them. Let me see. Doesn't one of his sisters live in Provo? Or is that Salt Lake. I can never keep those two cities apart."

"They were talking about Maria." Nora raised her voice. "There's no use in denying it, Mother. Maria and Kevin are going to be parents." They went out a side door to the church parking lot.

Rebecca Fairchild stopped. "Didn't you listen to Reverend Miller's sermon today?" she said urgently. "Didn't you hear what he said about Thomas? I know it's not easy. I just lost a husband. Do you think I don't know what it is to doubt the word of God? Why did He have to take Earl so soon? We were going to grow old together. But you, you're young. You have your whole life in front of you."

They got in the car and Nora sat in the passenger seat. "That's right, Mother," she exploded. "I have my whole life ahead of me but I don't have forever. Maybe you were having a vivid dream about Kevin and me getting married. Maybe you just wanted it so bad you thought it was God talking to you."

"God often talks to me in my dreams," Rebecca said quietly. She started the car. "That doesn't mean they are any less true than if he spoke through a… a… burning bush. He has never steered me in the wrong direction." She shifted into "drive", made a U-turn in the parking lot, and headed for the exit.

"But what if you are wrong this time? You thought your husband wasn't going to die, but he did."

"I can't read the mind of God, darling. All we can do is to have faith."

The word "faith" stuck in Nora's mind. When she was a little girl the word had meant hope and something to strive for, but today it was being used against her. Nora looked at people, still flowing out of the church, and wondered how many of them really had faith. Reverend Miller was outside giving a pat on the back, a smile, a laugh, or maybe a word of advice to the children, the parents, and the old people as they filed by. Ahead of Nora, traffic was backing up at the stop sign. The scene hadn't changed much since she was a little girl, she thought. But now something seemed different. She felt strangely separate from everyone else.

She put on her sunglasses and turned to her mother. "I'm tired of being alone."

19

The Wasteland

ZACK HAD A SPRING IN HIS STEP when he returned to
Silverman IV to start his first shift after his weekend with Margaret
in the Sawtooth Mountains. He peered down the hall and noticed
a new patient, a young, good looking man with wavy black hair.
Zack entered the nursing station just as they began shift report.

"Who's the new patient?"

Irene glanced up from a chart. "What new patient? We don't
have a new patient."

"I just thought I saw one, a young man. ..wavy black hair." He
hated feeling confused in front of Irene. She made him feel stupid,
but this morning was different.

"That must be Joshua. He just got a haircut and a shave this
weekend."

Zack feigned amazement. "Well I'll be damned. You mean we
actually created a positive behavior pattern in a patient?"

"I'm afraid so," said head nurse Marla wryly. "Let's begin the
report." She ran through a list of patients as the night shift commented on each one. When they came to Joshua, Marla removed a
form from his chart and held it up.

"We have a petition for release from Joshua's lawyer. They're having a court hearing next week and I'm going to recommend we transfer him off the unit. With proper follow-up of course."

The unit psychologist, Bob Winkelman, a timid researcher with scant clinical expertise who had used his seniority to transfer to Silverman IV, looked up from a big pile of charts on his lap. "Of course, of course, by all means," he chimed in. Suddenly the charts slid off his lap. "Oh shit." he attempted to swat them back into place but they tumbled onto the floor anyway.

Marla looked away and rolled her eyes. Zack helped Winkelman pick up the charts. Irene stifled a laugh.

Marla tried again. "He's been status four for three weeks and I think the medication is working. His mother is eager to get him home and… let's see… Bannock County Mental Health is ready to schedule a follow-up appointment as soon as he's released."

"Where's he going from here?" asked Winkelman.

Marla stared at him slack jawed. "Step-ping Stones, Step-ping-Stones. We'll discharge him to Stepping Stones where they can observe him in a less restrictive setting. Maybe take him on some field trips."

"Less restrictive setting. Yes, yes. That sounds very good." Winkelman bobbed his head. "I think Joshua will do well there."

Marla wore a pained expression. "Are there any more comments?"

Seeing none, they staffed a couple more patients then waited for the breakfast trays to come.

Later in the day, Zack approached Joshua.

"How's it going?"

"Pretty good."

"That's what I hear. We're going to try and get you transferred off the unit."

"I know. They told me this morning."

"How do you feel about that?"

"I think I'd like to try it."

Zack chose his words carefully. He didn't want to sound confrontational.

"I think you've done great with our program, but how do you feel about being back home?"

Joshua smiled sheepishly and pushed his hands in his pocket. "Well, to tell the truth, it's kind of scary. What happens if I go off my nut again?"

"Get some help," offered Zack. As soon as the words were out of his mouth he realized that it sounded too simplistic. By the time he "went off his nut" it would be too late to get help. "I mean, go talk to your doctor. Maybe he can adjust your medication."

"Yeah, I'll talk to my doctor before it gets too bad."

"*If* it gets too bad," emphasized Zack, doing his best to smile.

"Let's try to be positive about things."

Zack patted Joshua on the back and continued down the hall thinking he should have handled Joshua differently. Maybe he should have let Joshua figure out what to do on his own. Zack despaired. *I'm not doing anyone much good. Many of the discharged come back. The unit is becoming a holding facility for the chronically mentally ill.* He told himself it was just a job, but that attitude stripped him of his spirit and reduced him to being no better than the lifers—the Irenes and the Winkelmans and the Marlas who merely showed up for a paycheck.

He meandered into the nurse's station. No one was there. He lit a cigarette and plopped down in a chair. He yearned to make a difference in someone's life. Maybe Joshua would control his mental illness because of something he had done. Maybe Billy would finally accept some small amount of responsibility for his predicament. There was hope but it was slim.

After work, Zack drove to Margaret's house. She met him at the door wearing a yellow terry cloth sun outfit with a teardrop shaped neckline that exposed her cleavage. She gave him a big hug and a kiss and invited him in.

Zack heard meowing coming from the kitchen. "You didn't tell me you had a kitty."

Margaret hurried into the kitchen and returned with a small black and white kitten. "I just adopted him last week."

Zack smoothed the fur on its head and it began purring.

"I think he likes you," said Margaret.

"I like cats. I've got one of my own. What's his name?"

"T.S."

"What's the T.S. for?"

"It's for my favorite poet, T.S. Elliot."

"He wrote *The Wasteland,* didn't he?"

"That's my favorite poem," said Margaret beaming.

Zack winced. He recalled the dreary poem he had read in a literature class. It contained all kinds of obscure references he was unfamiliar with and phrases in Latin, or was it French? He even remembered that Elliot married a woman with mental health problems.

Zack picked up T.S and held the cat up to his face. "Well, well, you're a very talented kitty." He handed T.S. to Margaret and she put him back on the floor.

Margaret took Zack by the hand. "Come on in here. I'm hoping you can help me with this."

She led him into her bedroom where a half-filled waterbed, its sides sagging inward, took up most of the space. "My landlord dropped it off last week. It was free, but I've had trouble filling it up."

The crumpled bed was encased in a dark wooden frame. "What did you do with your other bed?"

"I didn't have a bed."

"You mean you slept on the floor?"

Margaret looked away. "I don't deserve a bed."

Zack gently placed his hands on her shoulders. "Does it have something to do with the abortion?"

Margaret raised her head. "I'm sorry but it's with me all the time. In the Catholic Church we do penance when we sin." She took a deep breath. "I decided that my penance was to sleep on a hard surface until God gave me a sign."

Zack was silent for a moment then asked, "Has he given you a sign?"

"Yes he has," she whispered softly. "You are the sign."

"Me? I'm the sign? Are you sure?"

Margaret led him back to the living room. They sat down. "When God speaks to me he always speaks through the heart," she explained. "He said that my time of penance had ended and that my soul would soon be fulfilled." She caught Zack's eyes. "I know this is a lot to take in." She kissed Zack on the cheek, rose and took two glasses and a pitcher from the kitchen. "Would you like some orange juice?"

"Ah... yes... orange juice would be good."

She poured him a glass then sat down, crossing her legs in front of him.

"Maybe I shouldn't have told you about the sign. You probably think I'm crazy."

"No, no. I don't think you're crazy. It's just that I'm not very religious."

"That's okay. I just thought it was important to share with you what is in my heart."

Zack smiled. *Alright, I'll play along with this and see where it leads.* He drew her closer and whispered in her ear. "Let's get that waterbed filled up."

He pushed himself up from the floor and helped Margaret up. They attached the hose to the bathtub spigot and pushed the other end into the waterbed intake valve then turned on the water. When it was firm, they disconnected the hose, plugged the valve and put the sheets on.

Zack embraced Margaret. "Are you ready to try it out?"

Margaret dimmed the light, reached into a drawer and brought out a bottle of massage oil. "I've been saving this for a special occasion. Turn over and I'll give you a back rub."

Zack stripped to his underwear and climbed on the bed. Margaret squeezed some oil on to her hands then began rubbing his shoulders.

"Do you want me to straddle you?"

"All aboard," said Zack, his face pressed into the bed. As Margaret straddled his back, the bed started shaking like a bowl of Jell-O.

He felt her warm crotch on his buttocks. She applied more oil and ran her fingers along his spine.

"I'm in heaven," Zack sighed.

After she finished massaging Zack's legs and arms, he rolled over.

"Now it's your turn."

Zack pulled the white string that held her top together. He applied some oil to his hands and massaged her breasts. Margaret closed her eyes and smiled as Zack leaned forward and kissed her nipples.

She rolled on her side, causing water beneath them to slop back and forth. Zack tried to turn with her, but the bed pulled him down.

"Help, I'm drowning," he laughed.

"Maybe we should put some more water in."

Zack hesitated to interrupt their lovemaking, if that's what they were doing. He wasn't sure anymore.

"No," protested Zack. "Roll into the middle and I'll get on top."

Margaret slid toward the center of the bed but when Zack went to roll over on her, she raised her leg and unintentionally kneed him in the groin. He cried out and collapsed into the fetal position.

"Oh, are you okay?"

At first Zack couldn't catch his breath. "I think I'll be all right. You just nailed me in a delicate spot."

"Oh, no, I'm sorry." Margaret stroked his cheek. "I'm sorry. Maybe this waterbed thing isn't going to work out."

"You may have something there," agreed Zack delicately straightening out his legs. Suddenly, he felt very tired. The hike, no sleep, and the long day finally caught up with him. He rolled out of bed and stood up. He didn't like leaving but he had to work in the morning again and without a good sleep he'd pay dearly.

"I'm sorry. I didn't mean to hurt you."

"I know you didn't. I'll be okay. I have to get some rest, though. You're probably tired, too." He hoped she was.

"I could sleep on the floor and you could take the waterbed."

Zack stepped into his jeans. "Not on your life. You don't deserve to sleep on the floor any more. Remember?"

"Do you really have to go?"

Zack put on his socks. He didn't enjoy disappointing her. For a moment he thought he might stay. He glanced at the bed. The waves rolled back and forth with Margaret's body gyrating in unison with them.

"I'd like to stay, but we can get together this weekend. Do you have the weekend off?"

Margaret's face lit up. "I'm off work on Sunday. You could stay over Saturday night."

"It's a deal."

Margaret slid off the bed and tied her top. Zack pulled his shirt on, circled his arms around Margaret's shoulders, then ran his fingers down her back. They kissed.

"I don't want to leave, but I'd better," he said, gently pushing her away. "I had a wonderful time."

"Bye," Margaret said quietly, trying to smile. "I'll see you Saturday.

As Zack drove home, he wondered if Margaret would misinterpret his leaving. *She has issues.* When he got home he fed Otis and fell asleep before his head hit the pillow.

———————◆———————

Nora drove a short distance up the hill and had lunch in a little park on campus. It was a warm sunny day and she found a bench beneath the tall cottonwood trees. She slipped a sandwich from a baggie, and took a bite. It was peanut butter and jelly; comfort food. Her mother made them for her and her sister when they were little girls. Nora washed down the sticky peanut butter with a can of grape soda. A little burp escaped from her throat, making her put her hand on her chest and look around to make sure no one was within earshot. She needed the solitude. She worried about the Doubting Thomas sermon, her mother's vision and Maria's pregnancy. She feared that she was losing her faith. Maybe God was testing her. The situation could change. Maybe Maria would miscarry.

She shuddered. What was she thinking? She would never wish such a horrible thing on anyone. Yet, there it was. She started to become dizzy, inhaled slowly then let the air flow out of her lungs. What if her mother's vision was just a fantasy?

She wished she could forget about her mother's prophesy and envied her friends who fell in love whenever they wanted. Sometimes their relationships didn't work out, but at least they had a choice. And what if she married someone else? Would God abandon her? Maybe if she convinced another person to put their life in God's hands, He would forgive her willfulness. Zack's face popped into her mind. Suddenly she knew what she had to do.

When Nora returned to the office, she called Zack. He reluctantly agreed to meet her for dinner at a local Mexican restaurant.

At six o'clock, Nora parked at the Loco Taco, near the edge of town, in the middle of Pocatello's small Mexican neighborhood. The restaurant was Zack's choice and, although Nora did not often frequent that part of town, the restaurant had a certain charm. The adobe walls were deep pink with wrought iron grates around the windows. In back, a small patio was shaded by a huge cottonwood. Its' large shiny leaves clacked briskly in the breeze. Zack waited at a table under the tree, smoking a cigarette and drinking a bottle of Dos Equis.

He saw Nora and waved.

"Well, well, I didn't think I'd see you again," he said after Nora sat down. "Would you like a drink?"

"Just a lemonade."

Zack liked that Nora wore the same tight glittery sweater she wore the first night he saw her in class. He decided to treat her like a friend, but when the wind blew the sweet scent of her perfume his way some of the old feelings came back.

The waiter handed them menus.

"Gracias," said Zack. "A lemonade for the lady and another beer for me."

Nora folded her hands. "So, how is your job going?"

"Okay, I guess. Actually, it's getting pretty damn depressing. When I started working there I wanted to help people, but now I don't know." He took a long draw on his cigarette and exhaled, watching the smoke drift away. "We're ending up with a lot of chronics. They improve for a while then regress back to where they were when they came in. Some we discharge, but as soon as they get off their meds they're right back again."

"I'm sure you can find a better job when you get out of graduate school."

"I don't know. I'm not sure I want to stay in the field." Zack picked at the label of his beer bottle. "Sometimes I just don't know what I want to do."

"I'm sure God has a plan for you."

Zack grinned. "Yeah, well if he does, he's not telling me what it is."

"Have you asked him lately?" inquired Nora leaning forward.

"I'm not the praying kind, if you know what I mean." He took another swig of beer.

Nora cupped her hand on Zack's wrist. "I know what you mean, but all you have to do is invite Him in." Zack warmed to the feel of her soft hand on his arm.

He placed his other hand on top of hers and leaned forward. "So how's *your* job going?"

"Will you come to church with me?"

Zack pulled away. Churches made him uncomfortable. Nora's eyes fixed on him waiting for a response.

"Now why would you want to bring a heathen like me into your church with all those other good God fearing people?"

"There are all sorts of people in our church. My mother used to say that just because you live in a garage that doesn't make you a car."

Zack gave her a puzzled look. "What?"

"Just because you go to a church doesn't make you a Christian," Nora said. "We all sin and struggle with doubt sometimes."

Zack motioned to the waiter hovering nearby. He turned to Nora. "Let's order. I'm getting the combination platter. I'd recommend the fajitas with guacamole. They're out of this world."

"Then that's what I'll have." Nora handed her menu to the waiter.

Zack leaned back and tapped out his cigarette. "I'll tell you a story. I was brought up as a Catholic on the south side of Milwaukee. My father was a lawyer and my mother… she raised the kids. When she was pregnant with her third child, she miscarried. She hemorrhaged and was in a coma for three days. Every day the priest came and prayed with us for her. I was twelve-years-old and believed that God would make her better. She never made it. I asked the priest why God hadn't saved her. He said her task on earth was finished and He called her home. I asked him why He took my unborn sister. Was her task here finished, too? He said God works in strange ways. My father… at least my father was honest. He told us he didn't know why she died. She just did."

"But God doesn't guarantee bad things don't happen, all He can do is to give us the strength to deal with them."

"People use religion as a crutch. That's all there is to it," said Zack flatly.

"So what's wrong with a crutch? Don't we all need something to help us through life? Something to give us hope?"

"It's a false hope." Zack broke a chip in half. "What's going to happen is going to happen. It doesn't matter what you hope for... or even what you pray for."

On the other side of the patio a little girl with dark hair and a white dress giggled as the waiter set a cake on the table in front of her. Everyone sang "Happy Birthday" to her in Spanish, then cheered when she blew out the candles.

Nora smiled. "Someday I hope to have a family of my own."

"Not if God decides he needs them in heaven."

Nora's smile was replaced with a frown. "How can you say that?"

"I was just thinking about my unborn sister."

"I'm going to pray very hard for you."

"Yeah, that's what the priest said." Zack jammed his cigarette into the ashtray. "What's with you? You're a beautiful woman with a mind of your own who still believes in all this mumbo jumbo about God telling your mother who you're going to marry. I mean you're not a child anymore."

Nora felt her belly tighten. She could hardly get the words out of her mouth. "I... I... I have faith that God wants the best for me, that's all."

"Well, if he wants the best for you he wouldn't have put you in the position where you're stuck with waiting for someone to become available for possibly the rest of your life. Don't you see you've got other options?"

She knew she had other options, but at what price?

"God always gives us free will. We can follow him or we can turn our back on him. It's our choice."

"Jesus Christ," exploded Zack. "I'm not asking you to turn your back on this God of yours. I'm just saying that your mother could have been wrong. I'm sure she believes in her vision, but you don't have to."

Nora broke out in tears. "I just wanted to have a nice dinner with you," she sobbed. She dabbed her eyes with a napkin then ran from the patio. Zack pushed his chair back and was about to chase her down and apologize, but changed his mind. *She needs to hear the truth.* He sat back down and lit another cigarette. The waiter showed up with their food. "Sorry, amigo," he said flatly. "The lady won't be joining me."

20

Identify the Emotion

THE FIRST SOUND Zack heard Saturday morning was the buzz of his window pane caused by the vibrations of a freight train passing in back of his house. He rolled over and looked at his clock. It was 10 a.m. Otis jumped up and sat on his chest like a sphinx. "How are you doing, buddy?" said Zack, stroking Otis's soft fur. Otis closed his eyes and purred. Zack started thinking about Nora.

Too bad she got upset... had to defend myself... trying to convert me again, like after Mom died... priest would come around every week with his sad eyes... all part of God's plan... Shit, I wanted to punch him... now Margaret thinks God released her from... what did she say... her penance for getting an abortion? Zack rolled his eyes. *How do I get hooked up with these women?*

Zack stretched and took a deep breath. Otis yawned.

"Okay, Otis, time to get up," said Zack, throwing off the covers. Otis headed for the cat litter box and did his business while Zack heated up some water for coffee. He put on some jeans, then took the kettle off the stove just as it started to whistle. He dropped a teaspoon of coffee crystals in the cup, poured in some hot water, then filled up Otis' bowl with dry cat food.

He brought his coffee cup into the living room, sat on the couch, and began thinking. *What if I started going to church... no, no... I couldn't do that... but what if I did. Then religion wouldn't be such a huge problem. Isn't that what most men do? They go to church to please the women... just go along to get along. Shit, I've been living out here too long... my mind is getting soft.*

Zack fired up a cigarette then flipped on the TV. He ran through the channels but nothing interested him. He took a sip of coffee and then another drag on his smoke. He had switched to Kools. The minty, suddenly sickening taste, coated his mouth. He snuffed it out and took a long sip of coffee. *Maybe I'll go back to Marlboro. Maybe I'll become a church mouse and join a Unitarian Church or something like that... lots of agnostics in the Unitarian Church. Then at least I could say I belonged to a church.* He chuckled and walked back into the kitchen for some cereal. *Settle down, become part of the community, have some kids.*

◆

Zack called Margaret several times but there was still no answer, so he decided to drive to her house. He looked forward to feeling her in his arms. Her car was in the driveway. He knocked several times and was about to leave when Margaret came to the door wearing a tee shirt and shorts. Her thick brown hair spilled onto her shoulders. Zack gave her a little hug, but she didn't respond.

"I called, but no one answered," he said, unsure of what to say next. "Last week you wanted to get together Saturday night...maybe take a hike Sunday."

"Oh, come in," she said in a monotone. She twisted the back of her hair, secured it with a rubber band, then turned and gave Zack a forced smile. Her face looked swollen. She led Zack into her living room, and sat on the floor with her back to the wall. Zack sat cross legged opposite her.

"You still want to take a hike, right?" said Zack.

She avoided looking at him.

"I don't know," said Margaret. "It's not you. I really like you but..."

"But what?"

"When you left here last week I felt like I would never see you again."

Zack held out his arms. "Well, here I am."

"I know but when Ernie and I were married he used to go away camping by himself for long weekends. He said he had to get away to clear out his head, but when he came back he seemed distant. Pretty soon after that we split up." She cast her eyes to the floor and didn't say anything.

What's going on? A week ago I was a sign from God, now she's cold to my touch. Better try a simple reflection.

"So when I left, you thought we were breaking up like, what happened with Ernie? Is that it?"

Margaret raised her head. She had a haunted look in her eyes. "It wasn't a thought. It was a feeling. It's like when I was a little girl. My mother had always wanted a boy and blamed my father. One day after Dad and I came back from a movie, they had a big argument. She accused him of not staying home enough and working on the house, but I knew it wasn't that. I think she always felt she was competing with me for his attention. I went into my bedroom and covered my ears with a pillow, but I could still hear them. It was terrible. Then I heard a door slam. He was gone. A couple days later he called and told me he had rented his own place."

"Did you ask to move in with him?"

Tears came to Margaret's eyes and her voice began to quiver. "I blamed myself for their break-up. I thought there must be something wrong with me. I didn't want to hurt him again."

"And you carried that around with you for a long time."

"I still do." Margaret got up, grabbed a tissue and blew her nose. "I'm really a mess. I'm sorry, but I don't think I'd be much fun. I need some time to be alone."

"Are you sure? I hate leaving you like this. Maybe we could take a drive and talk it out."

"That's okay. I'd only bring you down."

Margaret walked him to the door and gave him a friendly hug. "We can talk later," she said. Zack kissed her on the forehead and left.

As Zack drove away, he glanced in the rear view mirror and wondered if he would see her again.

With Margaret out of the picture for the weekend, Zack got together with Reverend Miller to tape record a counseling session. The tapes were used to persuade faculty that the student had the right stuff to become a professional counselor.

Tim lived with his wife in a ranch style house overlooking the city. Zack drove up the serpentine road, glancing at the valley and river below. It was an impressive view. He envied Tim and wondered how a campus minister could afford such a prime spot. He parked in the driveway and rang the doorbell. Tim came to the door dressed in shorts and a football jersey, followed by a white poodle that began barking as soon as it saw Zack.

"Don't worry he doesn't bite. Come on in."

Reverend Miller pushed the door open and Zack squeezed in. The dog retreated to the living room. Zack felt lucky to have a friend who knew something about counseling. Although Tim had been a minister for twenty-five years he wasn't out to convert anyone. He had been active in the Free Speech Movement at Berkley,

California, in the early 1960's, and had been a high school teacher before becoming a man of the cloth. As campus minster, he worked with all faiths and had a liberal outlook on life. Zack felt they were equals, just two grad students trying to get their degrees.

They poured some coffee and walked around the outside of the house, past a nicely landscaped patio and through the doorway to Tim's office. He had a big desk covered with books and files. The carpeting was threadbare in spots and the shade from the trees outside darkened the room. They talked a while about professors, Tim's conference, and the program. Finally they flipped a coin and Zack went first. Tim stood the microphone on the table and turned on the tape recorder.

"So, Zack do you want to talk about something today?"

"Yeah, I've been going through some hassles with women lately and I'm not sure why I get myself into these situations but I always do for some reason… I don't know…"

"Have you noticed a pattern in your relationships?"

Zack took a sip of coffee. "What usually happens is that I'm attracted to a woman because… you know… because she's kind of hot and I want to have sex. Do you think that's a bad thing?"

"It doesn't matter what I think. It's what you think that counts."

"Touché my friend," said Zack with a grin. "Sometimes I think I get myself into situations where I'm going out with a woman just to get laid when I should be looking for someone I have something more in common with."

"Do you think sex might have been an obsession there for a while? Is that what you're saying?"

"Did I ever talk to you about Anitra?"

"No I don't believe you ever mentioned her to me."

"We lived together for a while in Wisconsin, before she committed suicide. I tried to help her. She suffered from depression but there was nothing I could do." Zack stared into a corner avoiding Tim's eyes.

"Did you have a sexual obsession with her?"

"Why the fuck do you ask that?

"Because we were talking about sexual obsessions and then you mentioned Anitra.

"I loved her and she loved me. That's the last time I really loved anyone…. I think… I don't really know… maybe I've loved some women but it seems it never works out, so I just concentrated on getting laid as much as I could."

"And nothing else," added Tim.

"And nothing else. I got into all these relationships based on… you know… wanting sex. Sometimes I'd fall in love, but it wasn't right, not deep down… I'd learned that a long time ago."

"You think it was a sexual relationship more than anything else?"

"I became really dependent on them. Love and sex got mixed up together. But you know… after sleeping with them for a while I start feeling… you know… I started feeling love for…"

"Or dependency…"

"Or dependency…yeah…"

"Love becomes dependency rather than love, if that's what you were going to say."

Zack leaned against his fist and scowled. "Well put it like this. I depended on them for love."

"You mean for sex."

"Oh…yeah." Zack chuckled. He shifted position then lit a cigarette. *I thought this was going to be easy, just make a freakin' tape. Now I'm making a fool out of myself.* He took a long drag, then blew the smoke toward Tim.

"This love you felt was a kind of intense dependency."

There was a long pause as Zack tried to sort out his feelings. "I don't really know… ah… dependency was…I think I felt love… or shit, maybe I never felt love. I don't know. I mean I think I did. As far as I know I felt love. I said I loved them." Zack picked up a pencil and started snare drumming on the table top. "It was a feeling I had at the moment."

"Was it an emotion?"

"Yeah, an emotion. Yeah."

"Can you identify the emotion?"

"Identify the emotion?" Zack squirmed again in his chair and took a long draw off his coffee.

"Identify the emotion? What do you mean 'identify the emotion?'"

"Love is pretty broad. It comes in many varieties."

"Yeah," said Zack flatly. *I'll bet I sound like Frank at the hospital… a schizophrenic with blunted affect… am I really that out of touch with my emotions?*

"There are different kinds of feelings. Could you identify them?"

"Oh… okay… ahh… kind of feeling warm and not alone and enjoying their personality."

"Enjoying just being with someone?"

"Well, you know, that touching and talking and just knowing someone cares."

"Cares for you?"

"Yeah, for me, but I don't know. It seemed like there was always some major disagreement in lifestyle. I think if I could find a woman with the same basic outlook on life that I do… I don't know."

"So you even became afraid of these women who cared for you. I remember you telling me once that you felt distance, even though they cared for you. Maybe there's something that blocked your returning their care?"

Zack took a deep breath and focused on Tim sitting behind his large desk, barely visible in the late afternoon shade of his office. *How long is this torture gonna last?*

"I guess so," said Zack, brushing off the question.

The tape recorder stopped. "Just a minute," said Tim. "I'll change sides. I think we're getting into some fertile territory."

"That's okay. I have some errands to run." Zack downed the last of his coffee. "Pretty good tape though," he said. "I hope it gets you a sponsor."

"Yes, I hope so," smiled Tim. "Next time you counsel me, I've got lots of grist for the mill."

Yeah, sure, thought Zack. *I can't wait to bust your chops.*

———————◆———————

Even though he was tired Zack had trouble sleeping that night. He sensed that leaving Margaret Saturday night would have repercussions. He was right.

Tuesday morning he received an email from Margaret.

> *Dearest Zack,*
>
> *I hesitate to send this email but I want you to know what's going on inside of me. As far back as I can remember, I've always dreamed of having someone to love and care about, of having a home and a family. But as I grew up I began to realize that I could never have that because I was so bad,*

awful and despicable. Oh, Zack, I hated myself so much because I wanted things that I was so incapable of ever getting.

The last few years have been like Hell. I'm getting stronger, but I realize that those basic feelings of worthlessness and inadequacy are still very deep inside of me. I've never felt more loving since knowing you but it has to be trying for you to be involved with me.

At times I feel there's something very wrong with me. So for this reason I can't see you anymore. It breaks my heart but I love you so much I can't bear to put you through the pain.

> *Hoping You'll Understand,*
> *Margaret*

Zack stared at the message for a long time. It didn't make any sense to him.

"What the fuck is this?" he said, looking up at Otis who was perched on the back of the couch. Otis yawned.

Zack read it again. *Which part of it is true? How could Margaret love me but still want to break up? But here it is.* He read the message again, but decided not to respond. He didn't know what to say.

Thursday he saw Margaret in group therapy class but she avoided his eyes. After class, he tried to switch groups but it was too late.

He would have to deal with it. When Margaret didn't show up for a class two weeks later, Zack asked the group for help. He had rehearsed his soliloquy and felt confident he could discuss the breakup with minimal emotional trauma. After all, it was only a class.

Zack raised his hand.

"Yes, Zack?" said Bill, a doctoral student who was facilitating the group.

"Just in case you don't know," Zack began, "Margaret and I broke up a couple weeks ago and I'm still trying to figure what went wrong. When we met, we had a lot in common. We were both from the Midwest and liked to go hiking together. We both wanted to help other people and that's why we enrolled in the counseling program but..."

"You don't seem upset about it," interrupted Bill.

Zack glanced up. "Well, sure I'm upset."

"What I mean is, you're just intellectualizing your feelings."

Zack darted his eyes around the circle. No one came to his rescue.

He stared at the floor. "Well... I... just... feel really bad and I need some help from the group... I don't know what else to say."

"Just sit there and get in touch with your emotions," said Bill.

"I can't. Everyone is staring at me."

"Just shut your eyes for a minute."

Zack closed his eyes and let a wave of sadness well up in his throat but choked it back. "I usually do my crying alone."

"You are alone. Just think about it. You're alone and Margaret is gone forever. You will never have her love. Not ever."

When the sadness came up again, he didn't resist. Zack buried his face in his hands and began to cry. After he stopped, he took a deep breath and slowly opened his eyes, numb and exhausted.

Bill handed him a tissue. "I know it's difficult getting intimate with your feelings, but is very important if you want to help others."

"I'm not sure I want any more intimacy," Zack said quietly.

"What kind of a relationship do you want?"

Zack thought about his conversation with Tim. "I guess a nice comfortable sexual relationship will do for now."

"Still afraid of intimacy," said Bill with a sarcastic smile.

"Yeah, maybe you're right," said Zack. He didn't want to argue.

After a couple more weeks, Margaret and Zack were able to exchange pleasantries before and after class. After the ninth group session, Zack wrote in his journal, *"This being in a group is really hard for me. I got the feeling today of wanting to withdraw, wanting to say, 'Screw all these problems, I don't want to deal with them.'"*

He turned the notebook in and the next session it came back. *"Congratulations,"* Bill wrote. *"You finally got out of the descriptive past and moved into the realistic present. Recognizing where you are and how you feel is really an important step. I wonder if you want to withdraw because of not wanting to help others or of not wanting to help yourself."*

Zack wondered too. He became obsessed with emotional planes and arcs and variations...feeling sadness and joy, letting his emotions go and reining them back in, protecting himself then allowing himself to be vulnerable. He began to berate himself for not being able to feel the proper range of emotions then he berated himself for being too sensitive. He even began berating himself for berating himself. He came to believe that he had a block, a kind of emotional impotence.

Bill's last comment, scrawled across the bottom of the page was, *"Zack, sometimes I feel that you are so close to getting through your block and then sometimes you just seem to blank on it. I believe if we really want to enough, we can break through these things. Good Luck."*

Zack felt a great weight being lifted from his shoulders. He tossed the notebook in the corner and smiled, "Good luck indeed!"

21

The Temptation of Joshua

THE CHURCH WAS QUIET when Nora slipped through the vestibule and into the sanctuary. As she approached the altar her steps echoed off the dimly lit walls and the dark mahogany figure of the crucified Jesus appeared to grow larger. When she reached the first row of pews, she lowered herself into a seat, bowed her head, then fell to her knees. She looked behind her. No one was watching. This was the first time she was in the church alone and she felt a bit self-conscious. *What if someone sees me? What will they think?* She tried to clear her mind. She had come to speak with God. Although she realized that God already knew what was in her heart she whispered, "I come to you, Jesus, for help."

She could hear the pigeons cooing on the steeple and the quiet whoosh of traffic on the street. "I come to you for a sign." Her knee hurt. She shifted her weight backwards and smiled. *How much pain had Jesus felt on the cross? I can endure a little discomfort.*

Her mind drifted. She remembered waking up in a hospital bed when she was a little girl, after experiencing an allergic reaction to a bee sting. Her arm hurt. Nora turned to her mother who was praying over her. Tears were running down her cheeks.

"Why are you crying, Mommie?"

Her mother smiled radiantly and stroked her brow. "God has returned you to us."

A door slammed in the outer chapel. Nora jumped, then tried to refocus her mind.

"I need a sign. Please God, send me a sign." She thought of Zack sitting there at the restaurant, his wide brimmed hat casting a shadow over his face. *Could what he said be true? Could Mother be wrong? If she was, then why would God make me suffer?* It was clear to her that Zack didn't really believe in God. Then a disturbing thought went through her mind. *What if there is no God?* She shivered. *No, that was not an option. The world would not make sense anymore. If there is no God, I'm lost.* She asked again, this time more loudly, "Please Lord, give me a sign."

She looked up at the statue of Jesus. The mahogany had cracked and the crown had blackened over time. She noticed the chisel marks where the carver had sculpted the face and a knot in the wood was beginning to show on the cheek where the stain was fading. She cast her head down then looked back up and saw only a piece of wood.

Her knees were still hurting. She rose and slowly walked up the aisle, then wandered into the vestibule where she saw a poster: *"The Jesus Revival: Contemporary Christian Music."* Underneath,

"Jesus Has A Plan For You." There was a photograph of three young men with long hair dressed in leather fringed jackets. One of them looked like Zack. *Maybe this is God's sign,* she thought. *If Zack won't go to church with me, maybe he will come to a concert.*

Zack pulled the Starchief out of the parking lot at the State Hospital and headed home. It had been a difficult shift. He had called a code when Frank refused to leave the shower. After the necessary reinforcements arrived, they placed him in five-point restraints on top of a metal cot. Two male staff held down each limb as Zack placed leather cuffs around his wrists and ankles then locked them to the cot with a strap. For extra measure, he put a belt around Frank's waist. He hated doing that to Frank because he had begun to improve—his conversations were beginning to make more sense. But it was a painful reminder that patients could suddenly relapse without warning.

As he pulled onto Interstate 15, he noticed a pronghorn antelope with white neck bands and stubby black horns sitting on a rise near the road, just watching traffic pass.

Zack smiled. This is what he moved west for. As he passed, the antelope panned the Starchief. Zack waved. "Thanks. I needed that."

He adjusted his sun visor and headed out onto the desert, a long, flat expanse of volcanic dirt ringed with low hills that seemed to go on forever. He thought about Nora and how she was confined by her mother's vision. Even though he knew her vision was just her mother's wishful thinking. She was just a kid, actually. Yet, he found her naiveté appealing. *I could have handled it differently. Maybe had too much beer.*

When he got home, he plopped down onto his couch. Otis jumped into his lap and began to purr. "Hey, big boy, what have you been doing all day." Zack ran his fingers down his cat's back. Otis purred and kneaded Zack's neck with his paws, a free massage that Zack always luxuriated in. After Otis stopped, Zack went to the refrigerator, emptied a can of wet cat food into a dish, and placed it on the floor. Just then the phone rang. It was Nora.

He was relieved. "Hi Nora, I was just thinking of you. Hey, about the other night. I was out of line, had too many beers."

"I shouldn't have left like I did. I hope they didn't charge you for my dinner. I can pay you back."

"No, don't worry about it."

"I've been going through a difficult time lately. Do you still want to see me? I won't blame you if you don't."

"I don't know. I've been going through some rough times myself," said Zack, tapping out a cigarette. He rethought his statement. Maybe getting together with Nora would help him get his mind off Margaret. "Just let's not talk about religion, okay?"

"That would be fine."

Those words were music to Zack's ears. He lit his cigarette and blew the smoke away from the receiver. "I'll tell you something. You have to start thinking for yourself."

"I don't want to talk about that right now—maybe when I see you. I was wondering if you would like to go to a concert with me... at the church."

Zack shook his head. "Didn't we just agree not to talk about religion?"

"This isn't about religion. It's about three young men with long hair and buckskin jackets singing songs."

"Sort of like Crosby, Stills and Nash?"

"Sort of," said Nora. "Some of the songs might have a slightly Christian theme but it's nothing heavy. There will be mostly young people there."

Zack was suspicious. *Maybe she's trying to lure me into going to church with her. Aw, what the hell. It will be good to see her again.*

"Okay. When is it?"

"Seven o'clock tomorrow night. Why don't you meet me at the church?"

"See you then," said Zack.

◆

Nora looked at her watch. It was 6:30 p.m. and, although the church was just a short drive from her mother's house, she wanted to get there early and save an extra seat for Zack.

Her mother walked into the living room where Nora was putting on her coat. She had ceased dying her hair blond and now the brown strands had streaks of grey. She smiled. "Who are you going with again? I'm sure you told me but my memory is not as good as it used to be."

"A friend from the university."

"Oh, I don't think I know any of your friends from the university."

"I met him in one of my classes last semester," said Nora immediately regretting she had used the pronoun "him."

"Actually I'm glad you're going with a young man. I think the past few months have been very hard on you."

"Really?"

"Really. I hope you have a good time." She gave Nora a hug. "You'd better not be late. Just remember that everything will eventually work out according to God's plan."

As Nora walked to her car, she was glad her mother was not upset. Immediately she reproached herself. *I'm a grown woman. Why should I care whether my mother approves of someone or not?*

After Nora arrived at the church, she waited for Zack on the small patio outside. The sun was just setting and the Twin Buttes on the horizon were coal black. There was a chill in the air and Nora put on her blue jean jacket. She looked around. People were streaming toward the church. A young man with a beard and a girl in a long dress and a shawl walked past. A middle aged couple with prints of Jesus on their T-shirts smiled at Nora. *Where is Zack? Maybe he is delayed at work.*

She entered the sanctuary and located two seats up front. She checked her watch. Five minutes to seven and still no Zack. A young man with a beard sat down in one of the two vacant seats next to her.

"I hope this seat isn't taken," he said.

"No," said Nora, looking into the blue eyes of a handsome stranger. "I'm meeting a friend but he can sit on the other side." She turned away. He heart fluttered. *There is something about those eyes.*

"Bless you," said the stranger. He gently extended his hand. "My name is Joshua."

They shook hands. "I'm Nora. Nice to meet you."

At the front of the stage, the lectern had been removed and the three musicians were setting up. One of them, a young man with jet black hair and a goatee, was holding a large bass guitar. He wore a leather vest, faded jeans, and cowboy boots. The banjo player was younger with wire rimmed glasses and an elaborately embroidered work shirt. The other acoustic guitar player wore a harmonica strap and had a long red hair and a beard. There was still no sign of Zack. *Maybe he decided not to come.* She decided to make the best of it.

The lights dimmed and the musician with the embroidered shirt said, "Hi. My name is Matthew and we're the Ark Revival Band. Welcome to our ministry in the name of Jesus, our Lord and savior. Let us pray. Lord, we thank you for this fellowship and for this night. For those who have not accepted you, we pray that you will fill their hearts with joy. Amen."

Nora raised her head. Maybe it was better that Zack hadn't come, she thought. She didn't want to make him feel uncomfortable. She looked over at Joshua.

"Amen," he said and smiled. She smiled back.

"For our first number we're going to do something that reminds me of mountain climbing in the Sawtooth Mountains just north of Stanley," said Matthew. "It's called 'Closer my God to Thee.'" The song began with a banjo intro, then the others started in singing,

Closer my God to Thee,
Closer my God to Thee,
I'm getting closer to God,
Closer to God,
I'm getting closer my God to Thee

When they reached the third verse everyone clapped along with the music. Nora and Joshua joined in and soon they were swaying with the music. During one of the songs, Nora noticed that Joshua was silently mouthing words, rapidly moving his lips out of synch with the music. She thought it was a bit odd, but realized that he was probably saying a prayer. At, intermission they went into the lobby and Joshua poured them both a glass of punch.

"Let's toast," he said.

"To what?"

"To our meeting on this beautiful night."

They touched paper cups and laughed.

"Are you a member of the church?" asked Nora. "I don't think I've seen you before."

"No…Actually I saw the poster on campus and thought I'd check it out," Joshua said, smiling like a little boy caught playing in someone else's yard.

"Oh, you're a student?"

"Not really," said Joshua. "I'm just trying to get settled. What about you. Are you a student?"

"No. I'm a secretary at the university. But, I do take classes once in a while."

"I'll bet you're a Cancer," said Joshua. "I can just feel that you're a very intuitive person."

"Why, yes, I am."

"I knew it," said Joshua with a satisfied grin. "I just knew it. Let me see your hand."

Nora extended her hand. Joshua turned it over and began tracing the lines of her palm. Nora enjoyed his gentle touch.

"I see you have a long life line," he said. "It connects with your heart line so you will probably meet a man that you love and have a long life together. You're single?"

Nora blushed. She wondered again what had happened to Zack and hoped he hadn't had a traffic accident.

"Oh there I go again," said Joshua apologetically. "I didn't mean to embarrass you."

Joshua was still holding her hand when the lights dimmed. They went back to their seats and enjoyed the rest of the concert together. When it was over, they walked onto the patio.

"I wonder if you can give me a ride to campus. I… I'm staying in a shelter at the campus church until I can find a place," said Joshua with that little boy look on his face again.

She balked for a moment but since she met him in church she decided to go with her intuition. "Certainly, I'd be glad to give you a ride."

They drove toward campus. "What time do they open?" asked

Nora.

"They don't open until ten," said Joshua. "I can just sit on the steps and wait."

Nora didn't like the idea of leaving her new friend with the beautiful blue eyes to fend for himself. It just wasn't the Christian thing to do. "Why not stop over for some tea and I'll take you over there after they open."

"Oh, bless you," said Joshua.

"That's the least I can do for you."

When they got to Nora's apartment, Joshua sat on the couch while Nora began heating some water for tea. When Nora walked into the living room, Joshua was slumping forward with his head in his hands.

"Are you all right?'

Joshua looked up. "I'll be fine."

"Why not take off your shoes and relax," said Nora. She went to a closet, came back with a pillow and gently placed it at the end of the couch. "Here, lie down on this," she said, patting it.

Joshua slowly rolled into the pillow. Nora took off his shoes. The blond hair above his ankles rose slowly as she removed his socks. She felt a stirring inside of her. He reached for her hand and slowly pulled her forward.

"You are so beautiful," he said. "You are my angel." He kissed her and she responded. Joshua put his arms around her and she lay beside him. Passion filled her body. She kissed him again and again until suddenly he pushed her away.

"No, no… It's not right," he said, his voice trembling. He had a wild look in his eyes. "Why do you tempt me like this, Satan?"

Nora sat up. "What's the matter? Why are you calling me Satan?"

"Because Satan is using you to tempt me the same way he used Beth to tempt me. Don't you understand? Can't you see? He's all around." Joshua's eyes darted from corner to corner then back to Nora.

She put her hand on his arm. "It's all right. No one is going to hurt you."

Joshua swatted her hand away. "What do you mean no one is going to hurt me? Satan wants my soul. He wants to make me un-clean. He will stop at nothing."

My God, thought Nora. *What's happening?* A bolt of fear ran though her. She got up and ran to the kitchen. "Let me make some tea for you." She tore open a cupboard and fumbled with a box of tea bags. Her hands were shaking. She peeked into the living room. Guttural sounds were coming from Joshua's mouth. She heated up a cup of water in the microwave and then threw in the teabag.

"Do you like sugar with your tea?" she called out, trying to sup-press the quiver in her voice. When Joshua didn't answer, Nora placed the cup of tea on the coffee table next to him. His head was bowed but he was now silent. "Here," she said. "Drink some of this and you'll feel better."

Joshua raised his head and stared at the cup. Suddenly, he sent the cup flying with the back of his hand and shouted, "Do you think I am a fool, Satan? Do you think you can poison me with a cup of tea?"

Nora retreated to the kitchen but regretted her move. *How am I going to get out of here?*

"Why are you saying things like that," cried Nora. "I'm a good Christian. I only wanted to help you."

"Oh, Satan," said Joshua with a sneer. "You can't fool me again. There's only one way to stop you." He lunged at Nora and put his hands around her neck. "I will thrash the life from you."

Nora felt his fingers press against her throat and tried to break away, but he threw her into the wall. The impact stunned her and she fell to the floor.

Zack pulled his car into Nora's parking lot and turned off the key. He noticed her car and decided to see if she was home and apologize for not making the concert. There had been a fight on the unit and he was sent to the hospital, but had escaped with only a couple bruises and a scratch.

When he approached Nora's apartment, he heard the loud thud

of a body hitting the wall.

"Nora?" he called. "Are you all right?"

"Zack, help me," cried Nora.

The door was locked. Suddenly he heard a voice screaming, "Satan… you devil woman…. I shall slay you."

Zack stepped back and slammed himself into the door.

"Nora, I'm here," he shouted.

The door wouldn't budge. He tried again and again.

Nora screamed, "Zack, he has a knife!"

Zack stepped back again and heaved himself onto the door. The center bulged inward. One more blow and the door shattered.

Zack rushed in. Nora was on the floor, Joshua standing over her with a large butcher's knife. Zack picked up a pillow for padding and moved around to the couch. Joshua looked at Zack as a spark of recognition passed between them.

"Joshua?" cried Zack.

Joshua dropped the knife and ran out the door.

22

The Sly One

DR. NEDERMAN LEANED BACKWARD in his chair, put his feet on his desk, and looked at the piles of books and papers jammed in the corner of his living room. "Twenty-five years," he murmured. "Twenty-five years and this is all I have left." He smiled sadly. How many times had he told his clients that they had to be responsible for the consequences of their actions? Now it was his turn. He had cleaned out his office at the counseling department the week before. Now he was surrounded by nothing but consequences.

The committee had recommended to President Cole that Nederman either take early retirement or his contract would be terminated. Cole let Nederman choose.

The sun was low on the horizon, sending lazy orange and yellow rays through the window. Though the room was becoming dimmer Nederman didn't turn on a light. Darkness was more comforting. He didn't need to reread the letter from his wife's attorney. She was filing for divorce and wanted the house and half his retirement income. The proceedings of the committee were supposed to be confidential but in the small university community secrets rarely stayed secrets for very long. At first, after she confronted him with his infidelity, he denied it. It was all a big misunderstanding. She didn't buy that. All right, he said, maybe he had a momentary lapse of judgment. He apologized. They still had his retirement funds to draw from. They could live a good life together and he asked for her forgiveness. It was a desperate plea, but he was in a desperate situation. He hadn't been sure where she had gone when she stormed out of the house but now he had his answer. The thick half-folded mass of pages on his desktop had been delivered that afternoon by registered mail. They had barely fit in the envelope. He picked at the pile with his pencil like the carcass of a bird fallen from the sky.

Nederman lifted the receiver from the phone and called his son. He had tried calling Jason several times over the last week but no one answered. *Maybe Ann had gotten to him first.* He shifted his gaze to his computer screen which displayed a small island with two palm trees surrounded by crystal clear water and wished he could be there. He had hoped he could have retired and been recognized for his contributions to the field of counseling.

———————◆———————

Rebecca Fairchild hadn't had a decent sleep in days. She feared that she had been abandoned by God. Her husband had died, she had seen her daughter's future husband marry someone else, and now Nora had almost been killed by someone she met in church.

Even though it was late, Rebecca desperately needed to talk with God. She grabbed her car keys and drove to the church. Her hands were shaking as she gripped the steering wheel. She entered the sanctuary and walked down the aisle. When she reached the front, she knelt at the altar and folded her hands together. The room was empty except for the steps of the custodian walking back and forth upstairs. She wasn't sure how to begin. He might have already forgiven her because he was a forgiving and merciful God, but she needed to put her thoughts into words.

"Dear God," she began, "I ask your forgiveness for my sins." She stopped. Which sin did she want forgiveness for? Was it the sin of pride? She had believed herself to be a prophet. Was she wrong or did she just let Satan deceive her? Maybe she was guilty of something else. Why didn't God warn her against Joshua? Was God punishing her for her pride? She only wanted to serve God. She was a good person. Why had God forsaken her?

She tried again.

"I know I am a sinner, I have tried to serve you but..." She stopped. There it was again. What was preventing her from telling God what He wanted to hear? Her heart jumped at the sound of something scurrying around behind her. *Maybe it was a large rat. Or something bigger.* She turned and caught the glimpse of a dark form disappearing under the carpet. Tears formed in her eyes.

"Why have thou forsaken me, God. Why have thou forsaken me?" she said in a loud whisper. She began to shiver and weep. at first silently, then in great wailing sobs. She knew now that Satan was stalking her and that he would steal her soul and she would spend eternity burning in hell. Suddenly she felt a pull on her shoulder.

"Oh God," she cried.

"Señora, Señora." She opened her eyes and saw the face of the janitor.

"Are you all right?"

"I... I don't know. He's out there. Don't you see him?"

"Who is out there?"

Should I tell him that Satan was in the church waiting for me? That he is going to steal my soul?

"Someone," said Rebecca. "Someone who wants to harm me."

"I no see anyone."

"He's out there," insisted Rebecca. She began to cry. "He's out there. He's out there."

"Momentito please, Señora. I will be back." The janitor called Reverend Miller, but he wasn't home. The woman seemed to be in great distress, so he called the police department. He hurried back to the sanctuary. "Someone is coming to help you Señora," he said.

Rebecca grabbed his hand and kissed it, "No one can help me

now. Don't you see? God has…" She stopped. No, she should not tell anyone God had forsaken her. She must stay and do battle with Satan alone. She looked around the room. No visible sign of Satan, but she knew he was a sly one and would find her when she was alone. She heard a scurrying sound coming from the vestibule.

"Do you hear that?"

The janitor looked around. "Hear what?"

"Oh God, he's back," she cried. "Run, run. He's not after you," she wailed. "He's after me!"

Suddenly a dark apparition appeared in the doorway. She watched, unable to move, as it crept slowly down the aisle prolonging her moment of anguish. She crossed herself just before being blinded by a flash of light.

"Officer," said the janitor. "This is the woman I call about."

"Thank you. I'll take it from here."

"Ma'am… Ma'am?" he asked. "Are you all right?" Rebecca Fairchild's eyes were fixed wide open and her mouth was frozen in a silent scream as she knelt on the floor beneath the wooden Jesus who silently watched from above.

"Ma'am, can I help you?"

She turned to the officer and began to cry.

"What's wrong? No one is going to hurt you."

Rebecca grabbed the officer's arm and he helped her stand.

"I... I... I..." she began but never finished. She knew that Satan manifested himself in various forms and this policeman could be one of them. She dare not say anything.

The officer reached to his chest, depressed a button on his two-way radio, and called dispatch. "I've got a woman here who is having a nervous breakdown of some kind. I'm going to bring her down to the station and maybe we can find out what's going on. She's a white female, about fifty, conscious, but not responding to questions."

"Ten-four," said the dispatcher. "Do you have a name?"

"Negative. We can check her out at the station."

"Come on, Ma'am," said the officer, coaxing Rebecca up the aisle. "You'll be all right."

As Nora drove down the hill from the Pocatello Regional Medical Center, she looked into her rear view mirror at the gently curved silver exterior of the modern three-story structure as it disappeared into the brown sagebrush. She took a deep breath and relaxed. Her mother was going to be all right. The medication seemed to be working. She had been participating well in group therapy and was going to be discharged soon.

Nora turned south on Interstate 15 and headed toward the airport where her sister and brother-in-law were scheduled to arrive.

Sara and her husband Tom were flying in from California to help Nora pack and then to take care of their mother when she was discharged.

Nora parked her car on the ramp and ran inside just as the luggage began coming off the baggage carousel. She scanned the crowd and located her sister who was wearing a bright red blouse. She ran up to her and gave her a big hug.

"I'm sorry to give you such short notice," Nora apologized.

"Don't worry," said her sister, a tall brunette with short hair. "You sounded desperate."

"You've been through a lot," added Tom, a short muscular man with a wide grin who had just pulled their suitcase off the carousel.

"I have," said Nora. "I can't tell you how happy I am to see you both."

They drove to her mother's house and unloaded.

"Make yourselves at home," said Nora. "I've got to meet someone at seven o'clock downtown."

"Someone special?" asked Jan with a smirk.

"Yes," said Nora with a smirk. "Very special."

Zack was sitting at a table at the Taco Loco with two glasses of wine when he saw Nora come up the stairs. It was early January and he was wearing a ski jacket. He stood up and waved. As she came closer, he noticed that she wasn't wearing any make-up. He reached out and gave her a big hug. Though she wasn't wearing any perfume, Zack found her natural aroma very appealing.

"I've missed you," he said, kissing her.

"I've missed you, too. Sorry I'm late, but it's been a busy day. I just dropped off my sister and brother-in-law at the house and have to go back and pack."

They held each other then sat down.

"You said on the phone that you have something to tell me," said Nora.

Zack had rehearsed what he wanted to say for days, but now he was at a loss for words. Instead he remembered how his heart had starting thumping when he first saw her enter the class room, the captivating aroma of her perfume, her impassive almost regal bearing. He remembered their bodies touching and the longing he felt as she sat close to him in the car when driving through the foothills. He remembered how she had blushed when they met for the first time in the counseling office and the smoothness of her body as they were making love. And now he wondered, after their back and forth relationship, if he had the right to ask. Why not?

"I'm leaving town and I want you to come with me."

Nora's mouth dropped open. "But Zack, I've made arrangements with a friend in Seattle. She's going to help me find a job."

Zack reached over and took her hand. "I know. You told me that on the phone, but I don't want to lose you."

But Zack, where would we go?"

"I've got a brother in South Carolina. He just bought 80-acres of land and he wants me to help him sell it.

"What about your job at the hospital?"

"They're driving me nuts on the unit," said Zack, running his fingers through his hair. "I need a change. Besides, I just heard that they're going to transfer Joshua back to Silverman IV. They picked him up running down the middle of the street after I called 911. I don't want to be around when he gets there."

"I don't know, Zack. This is so sudden."

"I haven't stopped thinking of you ever since that day at the hot springs. I think I've fallen in love with you."

"Oh, Zack, I felt something for you too. That's why I told you about my mother's vision. I didn't want to lead you on."

"But don't you see? It's different now. We can start over. I don't know what's going to happen but you said yourself that there's nothing left for you here. Let's have an adventure together."

Nora was silent for a moment: "You're serious, aren't you?" She smiled and moved closer. "You know, I'm beginning to see that I was lost in my mother's fantasy. But now I have a chance to follow my own dreams. I just have to figure out what they are. One thing's clear: I need to get away. Maybe this is what God—"

Zack interjected "Maybe this is what you want."

"I think I do. But I also feel I owe you my life."

"You owe yourself a life and I want to be a part of it."

Nora smiled "This doesn't have to be the end of our relationship. I'll call you when I get to Seattle."

Zack shrugged his shoulders and sighed. "And I'll come and see you after we sell the land." He leaned over the table and gave Nora a kiss.

Nora raised her wine glass. "Let's toast to our future."

Zack picked up his glass and they clinked. "To our future."

About The Author

Richard Chamberlin has a BA in Journalism from
Columbia College in Chicago and has been a news-
paper reporter, freelance writer, psychiatric nurse, and
cab driver. He lives with his wife Judi in the small town
of Green Valley, Arizona, located just south of Tucson.

CPSIA information can be obtained
at www.ICGtesting.com
Printed in the USA
FSOW01n0325020315
5407FS